BETTER ANGELS

TOUR DE FORCE

STEVEN D. BREWER

Cover artwork design copyright © 2023 by Sleepy Fox Studio
sleepyfoxstudio.net

Published by Water Dragon Publishing
waterdragonpublishing.com

ISBN 978-1-962538-21-3 (Trade Paperback)

FIRST EDITION

10 9 8 7 6 5 4 3 2 1

CONTENTS

BETTER ANGELS

"**P**LEASE, MASTER," she implored from her knees. "Won't you please take me with you?"

She was kneeling in front of a dilapidated sign that once was garish, but now just looked sad and tired. It said "Little Angels", with faded, peeling pictures of smiling girls and rainbows. A man sat farther back, in a lawn chair under an umbrella. Behind was the spaceway that led to a docked freighter.

The incongruity of the umbrella and lawn chair on a space station was not lost on the passer by. He was a young man, only too obviously well-off, who was here in the Red Quadrant of the Truck Stop, slumming. He wore expensive, non-replicated clothes — you could tell from the slight irregularities of the fabric and stitching, if you knew what to look for. But they were soiled and he had quit shaving — or had never started — but could only grow sparse facial hair below his jawline.

"Please, Master," she continued, supplicating with her hands raised to him. "I'll do *anything* for you, if you'll just buy me."

The girl looked young. No longer a child, she was just starting to develop curves. But there was little left to the imagination as she wore only a sparkly, sheer negligee. And a thick, red collar round her neck.

She straightened her back and thrust out her chest, as he slowed, inspecting the merchandise.

"How much?" he asked the man.

"For her? 25K."

"Oh, you've got to be joking!" the passer by said, and started to walk faster. The girl collapsed onto the deck and started sobbing.

"Wait, mister! Wait!" the man called from his lawn chair. "How about 15K?"

"Five," the passerby said. "That's my final offer."

"That doesn't even cover my feedstock," the man said. "At least give me ten!"

"Seven."

"Seventy five hundred?"

The passerby went to walk on and the man called after him, "OK, OK! Seven!"

The young man returned, some currency changed hands, and the man snapped a leash on the girl's collar. She began to jump with excitement and clung to the young man's arm.

"This *Li'l Angel* is all yours," the man said with a leer. "Have fun!"

Two hours later, the young man was back in his mom's pinnace heading to a card game in the next spiral arm. He had undocked from the Truck Stop and, after he finished the calculations for the jump, he double checked the energy levels one last time.

"Master!" she called from the cabin. "I'm ready for you!"

He walked back, where the girl lay curled up in his bunk — her negligee now crumpled in a heap on the floor. He pulled the cover back when she suddenly whirled around, striking him in the throat with the ball of her foot. He fell to the deck writhing in agony, struggling to breathe. He heard her footsteps on the deck as she ran lightly to the bridge.

With his fading eyesight, he saw her expertly running her hands over the controls. Suddenly, a warning klaxon sounded and he heard an audio alert broadcast through the small vessel,

"Decompression warning! Decompression warning!" She had put the ship into maintenance mode and overridden the safety settings to open all of the vents.

A hiss became a roar as the cabin explosively depressurized. Objects swirled around the cabin as they were pulled loose, then dropped to the floor as the pressure fell to zero. The last thing he saw was the girl collapsing to the deck as the last of the air was sucked from the cabin.

An hour later, a large freighter appeared, drew the pinnace into a cargo hold, and then jumped to points unknown.

•　　•　　•

David walked down the docking ring in the Red Quadrant of the Truck Stop and, without even a glance at the pleading girl in the negligee and blue collar, went straight to the man in the lawn chair.

"Oh, no," the guy groaned, as David approached. "Not you again. You've been hounding me for more than a year! You already got me kicked off of every civilized station. And now I'm stuck here in this lousy back alley. But, hey! At least you can't get me kicked off here."

"You're a monster, Gaetz," David said, staring at the ground. "And I will never stop until you end this beastly trade."

The girl had followed after David and pulled at his shirt while she pleaded with him to purchase her.

"There's nothing illegal about what I'm doing," Gaetz said.

"How can you say that! Just look at this little girl!"

"She's not a girl!" Gaetz said angrily, then mastered himself. "How many times do I have to fucking tell you! She has no human DNA — it's clean-room biological engineering. She was molecularly assembled to spec and has a personality module. That's not a fucking person."

"I don't care what you say," David said. "Just look at her! Your brain knows that this is a little girl and you're a monster for treating her like this — for treating anyone or anything like this."

"Look. There's no-one on this station you can complain to that will get me thrown off, but you're a fucking pain in the ass," Gaetz said. "How about I just give her to you, huh? Maybe you can save her or free her or do whatever the fuck you want with her. But then, after you convince yourself, maybe you'll leave me the fuck alone."

Gaetz hooked a leash up to the girl's collar and handed it to David. The girl started jumping for joy and began clinging to David's arm as they walked back to his ship. David removed the collar and threw both it and the leash into the first trash receptacle they passed.

"What's your name?" David asked, uncomfortably.

"I don't have a name, Master. Yet!" she said, holding tight to his arm. "What would you like my name to be?"

"What do you mean, you don't have a name?" David exclaimed. "How can you not have a name?"

"I'm sorry, Master," she said, tearing up. "I didn't mean to make you angry!"

"I'm not ... angry," David said. "I'm just incredulous. How can you not have a name?"

"I'm sorry, Master! I'm sorry," she wept. She collapsed at his feet, sobbing. "I'll do better. I'll be good."

"No, I'm sorry," he said, scooping her up effortlessly and carrying her in his arms. "I didn't mean it was your fault."

"I know, Master," she said, wriggling contentedly in his arms. "I know you would never hurt me."

David closed his eyes for a moment, took a deep breath, and then walked ahead impassively. David really wasn't comfortable around people.

They walked down the spaceway and arrived at David's ship. He set her back on her feet and triggered the hatch. As soon as the hatch was a handspan open, she slipped inside. He could hear her running around inside shrieking with delight while he waited for the hatch to open enough to admit him.

"Master is so rich!" she said. "What an amazing ship you have!"

"It's not that nice," he said, looking down.

"Yes, it is!" she said. "This is a Xerxes Mark VII! This is a classic!"

"I guess some people like them," David said, temporizing. "Let me lay in a course for Cassandra. I know a woman there who might be able to help you."

"Have you decided what to name me, Master?"

"Just give me five minutes to lay in our course."

After completing the calculations, and entering the course, he locked the console while the ship automatically undocked and headed toward the jump point. He stepped away from the bridge and walked back to where she lay curled up in his bunk with her negligee discarded on the floor.

"Come out of there," he said.

"No, Master! Get into bed with me!"

He reached down and took hold of the covers. She whirled in the bed, lashed out with her foot, and caught him in the throat. He fell to the decking, strangling, as she sprinted for the bridge. He could hear her trying to input commands.

With difficulty, he got back to his feet and walked back to the bridge. After discovering that the controls were locked, she was trying a bunch of odd, seemingly random keypresses. David knew she was trying to break through the lock using known exploits against locked control panels.

"That's not going to work," he started to say when she turned and struck out at him again. This time he was ready. He snatched her up when she tried to kick him in the throat. She promptly bit his arm, drawing blood. No sooner had he dropped her than she whirled and kicked him in the head, then darted back to the controls and began frantically pressing keys again. David grabbed her and carried her, squealing and struggling, back to the brig and tossed her inside.

To call it a brig was an exaggeration: it was a storage closet with a barred gate that could be locked from the outside, as it now was, and could double as a brig when needed. The Little Angel paced back and forth just inside the gate hissing and snarling at him.

"I guess once you show your true colors, you don't bother trying to be friendly anymore," David said.

She shot her arm through the grate trying to get a hold of his clothes. David stepped back out of range. She resumed her angry pacing, shooting him positively evil looks.

He knew from past experience that the "Little Angels" did not exhibit a programming interface. All androids, whether biological or mechanical, were required by law to exhibit a public programming interface, even if locked, that would allow anyone to confirm their status and the responsible party: the owner or manager of the android. But it wasn't just a feature of daytime dramas for rogue androids to have their interface turned off.

For the next two days, while enroute to Cassandra, he tried talking to her, ordering her, pleading with her — even crying. But it was to no avail. She could not be reasoned with. She would neither eat nor drink, slapping anything offered to the floor. She continued to pace and snarl and shriek at him.

In desperation, he tried some educational videos, to see if maybe something could calm her down or elicit a different response. The first video, Jabbu from Muppyville, was of no interest. She continued to pace back and forth. He was really worried about her lack of drinking; she must be getting seriously dehydrated. He went to get her another cup of water.

When he came back, she was dancing. Dancing! He dropped the cup of water he was carrying in surprise. Then she started to sing. Her voice was astounding. It was on-key, pure, and — there was no better word for it — angelic. After several moments, entranced with her performance, he realized that she was responding to some kind of advertisement that was playing associated with the show. He went to look at the screen, but the song ended and, as quickly as she had started, the Little Angel reverted to pacing and snarling.

He grabbed his device, rewound the show by a few minutes, and started playing it again. Jabbu ended and then the advertisement came on. She immediately quieted and watched utterly fixated while a band of young girls wearing elaborate, brightly colored dresses came on screen. Once they started to sing and dance, she watched them intently until they'd been through the routine once and then she just ... joined in. She matched their words and movements perfectly.

He went back and got another cup of water. By the time he returned, the advertisement had ended again. He rewound it a second time and started playing it, but this time he interposed himself between her and the screen.

"Let me see! Let me see!" she pleaded. "I want to see!"

"Here. Drink this," David said. "Drink it all."

She drank the whole cup of water in one long pull. He stepped out from in front of the screen and her eyes drank in the sight of the girls dancing. She was enthralled. The cup slipped from her fingers and, once again, she began to dance and sing along with them, matching them motion for motion and word for word.

"Do you like this music?" he asked while she was still watching.

She ignored him while she was singing and dancing. Once the song ended, however, she shook her head and launched herself at the bars, snarling, and trying to snatch at his clothing.

He rewound the video again and stood in front of the screen until she started begging again.

"Is there any music you like even more than this?" he asked.

"PuzzyCure! I love PuzzyCure!" she said. "But let me see! Let me see!"

While she watched the video again, he looked up PuzzyCure and found that they were an idol group from a century ago. He downloaded a concert and started it up.

"PuzzyCure! PuzzyCure!" she shrieked with excitement. Then he stepped in front of the screen. "Aw! Let me see! Let me see!"

"Do you have a programming interface?" he asked.

"Yes," she said. "But it's turned off."

"If you turn it on, unlocked, I'll let you watch," he said.

He checked his device and, after a few moments, saw that there was a new programmable object in the area. He linked to it and then stepped out from in front of the screen. She basked in the view of the girls coming on stage with a beatific expression on her face. And when the music started, she began to sing and dance immediately, as if she already knew the entire performance by heart.

David began to scroll through her programming interface. She had a dozen personality modules in her stack, but they had all been overridden with a crude, single module on the top, and that module had no metadata associated with it. The basic physiology and language modules at the bottom were just the standard modules you'd find anywhere. But there were several layered in between them that identified a company that had programmed them: Magicorps.

He looked up the name and, after searching in archives, found an old news article. Magicorps had created a model of artificial human that could quickly learn song and dance routines. They had planned a series of galactic-wide tours with troupes of performers in magical-girl costumes performing as pop idols. Their goal had been to be able to respond promptly when a pop song became popular to meet the sudden demand for live entertainment. But that style of pop music had gone out of fashion, the company went bankrupt, and the scumbag selling the Little Angels must have gotten ahold of their design somehow. He had created — or, more likely, had paid someone to create — the crude overlay personality that made her act like a sex slave and then try to take over the ship.

He disabled the overlay. Then he deleted it altogether.

The girl suddenly looked around in shock and tried to cover her nakedness with her hands.

"Please, Mr. Producer!" she begged, blushing. "Please, can't I have some clothes?"

"Just a moment," he said, hurriedly, and made a few selections on his handheld device. By the time he walked back to the fabricator, the clothes were finished. He brought them back and handed them to her.

"Oh, Mr. Producer! How did you know?" she squealed, excitedly pulling them on. "A magical PuzzyCure dress and tights! Thank you! Thank you, Mr. Producer!"

"You can call me David," he said. "What should I call you?"

She cocked her head over, thinking.

"I don't remember my name, David," she said. "Can you give me one, please?"

"How about Zaza?" David asked. She nodded enthusiastically and whispered it to herself.

"Are you hungry?" he asked.

"Yes, please," she said. "May I have a Fun Meal?"

"You've got it, Zaza," David said. He made a quick selection on his device, walked back to the replicator, and returned with her meal. He opened the door of the brig and invited her to sit at the dining table while he continued to study her programming interface.

"May I please watch the video while I eat?" she asked.

"Sure," he said, turning the screen toward the table.

She ate happily, humming and pretending to conduct the music with her finger. David continued to study the programming interface. After she ate, she was sleepy, so he tucked her into bed for a nap while he continued to work.

"Aha!" he said finally.

After hours and hours of poring over the code, he understood what had happened. The overlay hadn't disabled the underlying code because it would have been too complicated to replicate a lot of the basic functionality. Instead, it had merely overridden it. That allowed the base functionality to continue to operate under certain conditions. But he had also discovered a very low-level block of code that bypassed the programming interface to allow the girls to link together to stay coordinated as a troupe. He thought it just might prove useful.

They emerged from their jump near Cassandra, but they didn't stay long. David made a call to an agent he knew, then reversed direction and started the jump back to the Truck Stop. On the way, he worked with Zaza to practice the choreography for a rather special dance.

•   •   •

One afternoon, Gaetz opened up the Little Angels storefront, dragged out his lawn chair and umbrella, and put a collar on the next girl to sell. Thus activated, she stood, leaving six others waiting. She followed him out and began trying to attract the attention of passers by. Traffic was slow. Gaetz looked across the docking ring and saw someone had set up a raised platform or stage with a sound system. That was unusual, but welcome. He rubbed his hands. A performance might bring potential customers!

Around twenty minutes later, some music started playing and a girl appeared on the stage wearing a colorful pink and blue dress with rainbow-colored ribbons and white tights. She started to dance to the music.

Gaetz watched her abstractly for a minute or two, then narrowed his eyes as he looked more closely. There was something familiar about that girl... Then he noticed that the collared girl who was supposed to be on display was standing stock still watching the performance. Then she too started to dance, mirroring the movements of the girl on stage. And then the other six uncollared girls, who were supposed to stay waiting on his ship, walked out as a group, and they also fell seamlessly into the routine.

Gaetz stood up, bewildered. He was still trying to figure out what was happening when the music suddenly shut off, mid-beat. He looked around in surprise as all of the girls turned toward him and began to run, their bare feet slapping the deck as they converged on him. The collared girl suddenly knelt down and one of the girls stepped up onto her back and sprang into a whirling kick attack that caught him full in the throat.

He fell to the decking choking while the girls surrounded him kicking, biting, scratching, and pulling his hair. Two girls grabbed his head and began repeatedly smashing it into the deck.

David let them go on — perhaps longer than was strictly necessary. But finally, he relented and started the music back up again. The moment he did, the girls stopped their attack and returned to dancing. He sent a command to remove the overlay from the troupe and then walked across the docking ring and offered each girl a PuzzyCure costume.

"PuzzyCure! PuzzyCure!" they squealed with delight. "Thanks, Mr. Producer!" David sent them across the concourse where they joined Zaza on the stage and continued to dance in perfect synchrony.

Finally, David went to Gaetz lying on the deck. He appeared to be in shock, only semi-conscious in a puddle of blood and a couple of scattered teeth.

"I wouldn't try your little scheme again," David said. "Any of your girls that sees their performance is going to go haywire, just like these girls did, and throw off their programming. So be thankful I'm letting you off this easy."

"You know this is assault," Gaetz croaked.

"Who assaulted you?" David said evenly. "The Little Angels that you were trying to sell into sex slavery? I'd like to see the judge that would find a judgment against them."

"I hope I never see you or a Little Angel ever again," Gaetz mumbled.

"If you get out of the business, I promise that you won't see me or the Little Angels again," David said earnestly.

David started to walk away, but then paused and turned back.

"Oh! But did you hear?" he said. "The Better Angels have a performance today that I understand will be broadcast station-wide to kick off their upcoming galactic tour. So I expect you'll be seeing a lot more of *them* in the future."

THE BETTER ANGELS
AND
THE VERY SCARY HALLOWEEN

THE LIGHTS SUDDENLY CUT OUT and there was darkness. There were a handful of screams in the giant space. Then the drums started up and the space stadium erupted with cheers. The bass picked up the beat. Then a spotlight stabbed down illuminating Zaza, wearing a pink-and-blue magical girl costume. She made a dramatic gesture and the stage lights came up, illuminating the rest of the Better Angels who struck a pose while the crowd went wild. They moved smoothly into their first number, a cover of a favorite PuzzyCure song.

The Better Angels had rapidly shot to galactic-wide fame as an idol group. They were non-human biological androids that looked like teen or pre-teen girls and wore distinctive costumes with short skirts and rainbow colored ribbons.

David, their producer, was in the office of the concert promoter arguing with him to keep to the letter of the contract. Word had gotten around regarding what would happen if someone didn't fulfill their contract with the Better Angels and so David did not have to actually make any threats. He received the full payment for the girls' performance with only minor grumbling. Later, before the show ended, he went to a nearby store to accomplish an important task and left with a small bag.

After the performance, the Angels were in high spirits returning to their starship, *Angels' Wings*. Once aboard, David set the coordinates, double-checked the energy levels, and then locked the console while *Angels' Wings* undocked automatically and began to head toward the jump point. David grabbed the bag and walked back to where the Angels were working off the energy after the excitement of their concert. Zaza ran up and grabbed his arm

"What did you get us?" Zaza asked.

"What did you get us!" they all started to ask. "What's in the bag?"

"Well, you have a choice," David said. "You can have a lollipop ..."

At this, half of the Better Angels cheered and half groaned.

"Or you can have bubblegum!" And then all of them began jumping up and down pulling at his shirt while he drew out lollipops and bubblegum, handing them out left and right while the Angels squealed excitedly.

"No malted-milk balls?" asked Nene.

"Did you want malted-milk balls?" David asked with surprise.

"No," she laughed. "I wanted bubblegum!"

David tousled her hair.

Before long, the sugar rush was over and the Angels started to get sleepy. Soon, they turned in after a long day in the spotlight. Later, David smiled to himself while he tiptoed through the quiet vessel that was now humming only with a normal ship's activity.

•   •   •

Tove came out of the rainy drizzle and, after passing through security, entered an elevator and pressed the top button. He presented himself to the camera, was recognized, and braced himself for the 15 minute express ride up to the very top of the CBMISonVeriNetfrimechyronaMAX building. He emerged into the quiet, paneled hallway that led to the executive offices of Mr. Besk.

He entered the office and Besk's receptionist, Miss Clit, requested he wait until Mr. Besk was ready. She was an attractive young woman with a severe hairstyle — and an expression to match — all poured into an elegant suit. Tove cooled his heels in the outer office, looking at awards for the various programs that Besk had been involved in producing, and trying not to stare at the shapely Miss Clit.

"Mr. Besk will see you now," Miss Clit said.

Tove stepped through. Besk's office occupied the entire top floor of the top of the building, and had floor-to-ceiling windows all the way around. They were above the clouds, where it was sunny, and you could see a half dozen other tall buildings protruding through the clouds.

"Did you find him?" Besk asked eagerly. "The man who was selling the Little Angels?"

"Bad luck," Tove said, considering carefully how to present the information he had in order to maximize its impact — and potential return.

Besk was visibly disappointed.

"The man you'd heard of, Gaetz, was involved in some scheme that involved stealing ships," Tove continued. "He was sentenced to re-education even before you hired me."

"Damn," Besk said. "That was our best lead to getting some of the Magicorps girls. Do you have any leads where Gaetz was making them?"

"It was probably his ship," Tove replied. "He had an old freighter big enough to house the equipment. But it was sold at auction almost the same day you hired me."

Tove waited a moment for that fact to sink in. Then he passed Besk a flyer that showed girls wearing pink and blue magical-girl costumes. "Do these girls look familiar?"

"Those are them! Those are Magicorps girls! Where did you get this?"

"There is a new act called Better Angels that is touring galactic wide. They mostly do old PuzzyCure songs, but there's been a huge resurgence of interest and they're making a big splash."

"You know what to do Mr. Tove," Besk said. "I must have them. I have a secret project in mind and nothing else will serve. Draw up a budget and spare no expense."

"Just to be clear, Mr. Besk. Wouldn't it be potentially cheaper to approach them openly and try to hire them?"

"That would tip my hand and wouldn't give me the control I need. I need to be able to install my own modules in their stack."

"That's what I thought, so I took the liberty of drawing up a plan, Mr. Besk," Tove said, bowing slightly and handing him a folio with both hands. Besk accepted it.

"As always, you're a professional, Mr. Tove. You can expect a nice gratuity in addition to your usual retainer. Let me know when you have good news."

Tove left the way he'd come, rubbing his hands. This was going to be like taking candy from a baby.

•   •   •

The alarm for the end of jump woke David. He tiptoed out quietly, to avoid waking the Angels, and took his seat on the bridge to check everything and to be on hand for the re-emergence into normal space. The countdown reached zero and David checked all the instruments. Everything was within normal parameters and he double checked the course to the Truck Stop. It was just visible on screen against the weird glow of the black hole and its accretion disk.

He turned on the station news feed and watched to see what events had happened during their absence. Zaza came out rubbing her eyes and put her little hands on his arm.

"Good morning, David," she said.

"Good morning, Angel," he said.

There wasn't much news. There had been a minor leak from a micrometeor that had gotten through due to a failure of the defense net and there was an investigation into how that had happened. There was a new resident of the Zoological Sanctuary — David couldn't quite tell, based on how the article was written, whether it was an inmate or staff member — a male NeoBoxer. David made a mental note to take the Angels to see or meet him, depending. The last article was a puff piece about today's Halloween celebration and encouraging tolerance among races that didn't practice the holiday for the kids' sake — and the advisability of having some candy on hand to prevent having tricks played on you or your ship.

"What would you like to dress up as?"

"What?" Zaza said, with a yawn.

"Today's Halloween. It's a holiday where children put on costumes and go door-to-door. They say, 'trick or treat' and people give them candy."

"Candy?" she said, her eyes opening wide. "They give you candy?"

"Mhm," David said. "You can get all kinds of candy that way."

"They just give it to you?"

"If you've got a good enough costume."

"What should we dress up as?" Zaza asked.

"I don't know," David said. "It sounds like something that you and the other Angels are going to have to decide for yourselves."

Zaza ran back and got the other Angels up and, over breakfast, they excitedly discussed and debated what costumes to wear. They considered all doing separate things, but decided that they wanted to do something all together. David smiled listening to them put their entire hearts into making this critical decision. Finally they decided and Zaza came out to the bridge to tell David.

"We've decided what we want to do," she said. "We're going to go as Icy Elsa and the Seven Androids."

"Isn't that the story where ..."

"Right! Icy Elsa is a princess who gets locked in an ice castle by her evil stepmother. And the seven androids take care of her."

"What kind of costumes do you want?" David asked. "You could make costumes yourselves. Or buy them. Or we could purchase the design and replicate them ourselves."

This required another round of shuttle diplomacy while the Angels debated the pros and cons of various approaches. But by midday they were docked at the Truck Stop and had decided to purchase the designs and replicate the costumes themselves.

David checked over the specifications to confirm that they were within the capabilities of their replicator.

"We could never have done this with the little replicator I had on the Xerxes Mark VII," he said. "But now we have Gaetz's huge replicator and so this should be no problem."

After the Angels had been rescued from the nefarious Gaetz, his tramp freighter had been sold at auction to pay his debts and David had bought it outright and renamed it *Angels' Wings*. But he'd had to sell his old courier ship to pay for it.

The courier ship had been fine for a crew of one or two, but was not comfortable for nine — especially when eight were girls who delighted in lengthy primping in front of the bathroom mirror. But the proceeds had been enough to buy the larger ship and accomplish a significant retrofit. They had retained, however, the large-scale replicator Gaetz had installed — and the recycler and other machinery associated with its operation.

David submitted the order, received the data, and scheduled the replicator jobs. He noticed an alert and checked it. There was a message requesting he come to an obscure law office — something about a possible lien against the title to Gaetz's ship. David sighed at the thought of having to go deal with people. He really didn't like dealing with people.

He went out where the Angels were jumping up and down watching the replicator create the costumes.

"I should be back in just an hour or two," he said.

They all ran over and grabbed onto him.

"Don't go, David!" Popo said. "Don't go! Stay with us!"

"I'll be right back, Popo!" he said, pulling away.

"Hey! I'm Sisi!" Popo said.

"You are not!" David said.

She stamped her foot, "How can you always tell?"

David just smiled, heading out.

"Bye, bye!" the Angels called, waving.

David slipped out the hatch, walked across the docking ring to the security checkpoint, and, after he was cleared, went on to the elevators. The Angels had reserved a permanent berth in the Green Sector, but now David needed to go to the Red sector — if the address he'd been given was to be believed. It was kind of an out-of-the way place. But, after jump, it was always nice to have an excuse to walk a bit. So David walked antispinward through the Blue sector until he reached Red. This area was less occupied and sketchier than the Green and Blue sectors. David consulted the map and walked down a long, dim hallway until he found the small elevator that led to the office where he was headed.

David got in the elevator and pressed the button. The doors closed and the elevator started up, but then stopped unexpectedly with a jerk and the lights went out. David felt around and tried pushing the other buttons, but there was no response. He found the emergency button and pressed that too, but it too was dead. He tried forcing the doors but they were locked between floors. He looked up to see if there was a hatch at the top of the elevator, but he didn't see how to get to it. He pulled out his device and tried to send a message, but found that there was no connectivity. At this point, he realized that this must be some kind of trap because connectivity should have been available in every part of the station, although the Red Sector was the least complete of any sector except Orange (which was still closed to ordinary personnel).

"Help! Help!" he called. There was no answer.

He sighed, sat down on the floor, and, after removing a shoe, he began to tap out S-O-S with the heel of his shoe hoping someone might hear.

•   •   •

Zaza was in the bathroom when she heard someone press the bell at the hatch. Three or four Angels ran to the door and triggered the hatch. Zaza heard a soft coughing sound and then screams. She peeked out the door and saw uniformed armed men using air pistols that seemed to shoot some kind of dart. She watched as Rara, running away, got shot from behind and dropped to the deck, unconscious. Zaza shrank back into the bathroom and looked around for a place to hide. She climbed into the bathtub and positioned herself behind the half-closed shower curtain. One of the men ducked his head in the door. Peeking out, she could see he was dressed as Truck Stop security. He looked around and then went back out.

"We've got seven," a man said into a device. "Yeah, I know there are supposed to be eight. Maybe one went with the guy? We're not seeing her here. Okay. Okay. Got it."

Zaza listened while the men gathered up the girls and carried them down the cargo elevator to the cargo bay. When she was sure they were gone, she ran to the bridge and tried to look at the cameras at the cargo doors, but the camera was dark — disconnected or painted over. She tried calling David, but there was no answer. Zaza turned around, tears in her eyes, and wrung her hands, wondering what to do. She was afraid to contact security. The men were probably just disguised, but she wasn't sure — she needed David.

The news was still playing. The first news item was that arrivals and departures from the Truck Stop were temporarily halted while they recalibrated the defense net to make sure it was tuned properly and didn't accidentally fire on arriving and departing vessels. Zaza watched and then saw the report about the NeoBoxer at the zoo. That gave her an idea. She was making a plan when the replicator dinged. Zaza went out and saw the Icy Elsa costume was finished. She changed into the costume and then grabbed something out of David's laundry. Closing the hatch behind her, she ran to the checkpoint, who passed her through quickly — and gave her a piece of candy for Halloween — and she ascended the elevator to the Green Sector.

She ran spinward, dodging the pedestrians, until she reached the Zoological Sanctuary. A young woman was just closing up. She was getting her keys out and holding the door ajar.

"Wait! Wait!" Zaza said as she ran up.

"Oh, I'm sorry, Miss," she said. "We're closed for the night."

"No!" Zaza implored. "I need to see the NeoBoxer. I need his help!"

"Oh, that's easy," she said. "He's coming with me tonight. Here he is! Say hello to Tau."

Tau pushed his way through the entrance. He was a massive example of the NeoBoxer breed, with tawny fur and a black face. Whirling around in curvets about Zaza, he shoved his black muzzle in her face and licked her mouth. She squealed with excitement and gave him a hug around his neck.

"He stole my first kiss!" she said, laughing.

"He's like that, Miss. Oh! Excuse me, but what's your name?"

"Oh, pardon me," Zaza said, turning to face the young woman and bowing respectfully. "My name is Zaza. I'm one of the Better Angels."

"Well, of course you are!" she said. "I'm Lusa. I'm a keeper here at the Zoo. Now, what did you need Tau for?"

"Oh! Oh!" Zaza said. "I almost forgot!" She pulled a sock out of her pocket. "My producer, David, is missing and might be in trouble. I was hoping Tau could help me track him. I brought a sock."

Tau sniffed the sock then barked sharply at Lusa.

"Alright," Lusa said. "He says he'll do what he can to help."

Tau began by sniffing the air and then ran toward the elevators. Zaza followed as fast as she could. Tau picked up the trail where David had emerged and he led Zaza at a rapid trot past the Gift Shop, the Casino and on into and through the Blue Sector. Tau overshot the hallway where David had turned off in the Red Sector and made another circling pattern until he picked up the trail again. Zaza ran close on his heels. They reached the end of the hallway where the elevator doors were jammed part way open with a piece of pipe.

"David? David?" she called into the opening.

"Zaza!" she heard very faintly from above. "Is everything okay?"

"No, David," she cried. "The other Angels have been kidnapped."

"Look around, Zaza," David called. "Do you see an electrical panel in the hallway. Maybe jimmied open."

Tau barked and pointed.

"I found it, David!"

"Look for a switch that's turned off and turn it on."

There were four switches turned off. Zaza turned them back on in order.

"OK. I've got power again," David called. "But the elevator still isn't working. Did they block the door open?"

"Yes, David! I'll close it!"

Zaza ran over and pulled the pipe out allowing the doors to close. After a short wait, the elevator dinged and the doors opened. David stepped out looking angry. Zaza flew to him and threw her arms around him. He crouched down so she could put her arms around his neck. Tau wriggled his way in between them and they all hugged one another.

"I was so scared, David!" she whispered in his ear.

"It's going to be okay, Zaza," David said. "We're going to get them back."

"Promise?"

David closed his eyes, swallowed hard, and said, "I promise. I will do whatever it takes to bring them back."

Then he stood up and looked Zaza up and down.

"Is that the Icy Elsa costume?"

Zaza twirled around lifting her arms.

"Isn't it wonderful!" But then she looked sad, "But I need my seven androids."

"Let's go get your androids," David said, then turned to Tau. "That is, if you're willing to help us a little longer." Tau barked and pointed the way back.

•   •   •

When they got back to *Angels' Wings*, David went to one of the smaller cargo bays and entered a very long combination into the panel. As the door opened, he crouched down with Zaza.

"There's something very important that only you can do. Are you ready?"

"Yes, David?"

"I'm about to do … something and, after I do this, I don't always know when to stop. I sometimes can't even tell good guys from bad guys. So I need you to tell me when to stop. Can you do that?"

"Yes, David. I can do that."

"Good. When all the bad guys are taken care of and the danger is over, you need to tell me to 'stand down.' Do you understand? Just those two words. But don't tell me too soon."

"I understand, David."

"I told myself I would never do this again. But here we are."

David stood, pulled out his device and, with a painful grimace, brought up an interface. With a few swipes, he re-enabled four modules.

Zaza watched, unsettled, as David's body language and facial expressions changed. His face grew hard and pitiless. His eyes lost their sparkle and looked dead. He stood differently and his movements became more feral, somehow.

"You're scaring me, David," Zaza said. "I don't like you like this."

"That's okay, Civilian" he said, with a flat affect. "I don't like me like this either."

He stepped into the storage bay and walked through rack after rack laden with weapons. There was an immense collection of different kinds of firearms: plasma guns, air rifles, magnetic rail weapons, and even some that used old-style chemical propellants. He selected a light railgun and some small grenades. He checked that the railgun was fully charged and loaded with metal. He adjusted it to fire low-velocity, soft bullets that wouldn't pass through bodies or light, interior walls.

"Tau," he ordered. "Lead us out. Civilian, stay behind me. If they have surveillance, they mustn't see you."

David triggered the cargo bay door. Tau picked up the trail and led them into the cargo passages. They bypassed the elevators up into the Truck Stop proper and continued down the docking ring. David concluded they were headed for another ship. In fact, Tau led them to the very next ship. David thought for a moment.

"Civilian," David said. "Go to the main hatch and pretend to trick-or-treat to get them to open the hatch."

"I can do it, David!" she said.

David slipped the railgun inside his belt and pulled his shirt over the butt. He checked everything. Then they took the elevator up to the docking ring. David and Tau stood to the side while Zaza rang the bell.

"What do you want?" said a gruff voice on the other end.

"Trick or treat!" Zaza said brightly, pirouetting for the camera.

"Oh. Right. OK," he said, triggering the hatch. Before the hatch was half open, David was inside. He dragged out the railgun and powered it up. Then he began to shoot. The first man, who was coming around the corner from the bridge, was dropped with only a quiet whine of the railgun and the slap of the projectile. The man fell with a neat hole between his eyes. David moved through the space killing as he went. A man sitting on the bridge with headphones was next.

Then he heard a voice from another room, complaining, "Whoever it was who set up these girls locked their wetware. We can't get access to their programming interface without a full wipe."

"Well, do it, then," said a voice obviously used to command. David passed that one and left him for last. He came around the corner and saw Lala lying unconscious on a table with a helmet on her head. Two technicians were sitting at the console of some kind of equipment on her studying the readouts. He shot them both through the head in quick succession. This time, the man in the office overheard the whine of the railgun and yelled, "Shooter!"

A man came out of the galley, spotted David, and shouted. He was shot next. Two men who were in the galley came tumbling out only to be gunned down before they could bring their weapons to bear. David returned to the office where he'd heard the commander's voice. David took up a position just outside the door.

"Tell me who was responsible and I'll make it quick," David said.

"I'm not telling you anything," Tove replied.

David stepped several feet back, then sprang forward and slid along the floor past the door on his side. Tove tried to shoot but wasn't expecting David to be so low and his shot went high. David shot Tove in the foot under the desk. It blew his shoe off and left his foot a mangled wreck of flesh and bone. Tove screamed in agony.

"I can keep you alive for years," David said, coldly, leaning up outside the door. "How many years do you want to spend begging for death?"

There was only the sound of Tove gasping and cursing for a moment.

"Jeon Besk," Tove said, finally. "He's the owner of CBMISon-VeriNetfrimechyronaMAX on Volpex."

David stepped in and, before Tove could react, shot him between the eyes.

David went through the rest of the starship quickly, but found no other opponents. Returning to the room where the technicians had been working, he popped open an interior door and found the rest of the Better Angels huddled inside. He raised his railgun.

"Stand down, David!" Zaza said from behind. "Stand down!"

David started trembling violently. He dropped the gun and doubled over with spasms. The Angels surrounded him, hugging him and crying. Zaza looked at Lala who was still lying, unconscious, with the helmet on. Tau leapt up and flipped a switch off on the device. Lala began to stir and wake up.

David, still suffering the after-effects of his transformation, led them down to the cargo bay, guided them out, then tossed a small grenade inside and sealed the hatch.

"What was that for, David?" Zaza asked.

"It's a nanobomb. It releases nanobots that consume organic matter."

"The bodies?"

"Yes. And all traces of us as well."

Tau led them through the cargo passageways until they reached *Angels' Wings*. David entered the code and led everyone in through the cargo bay. Still shaking a bit, he replaced the weapons in his armory and relocked the door. By the time he'd reached the bridge, he was mostly back to normal.

"Welcome back, David," Zaza said, tugging at his sleeve. "I'm glad you're you again."

"Me too," he said, then grimaced again. "Although I'm going to have to do that at least once more. But for right now, is everyone still up for trick-or-treating?"

The Better Angels squealed with excitement and Tau turned somersaults in the air.

"What can Tau go as?" David asked Zaza. She tapped her lips thoughtfully.

"He can be Veni-san, the reindeer spirit!"

While the seven Angels put on their android costumes, David replicated antlers for Tau and bags for the Angels to carry home their candy. Then they set off through the Truck Stop where the Angels and Tau would ring a bell, shout, "Trick or treat!" and strike a pose for the audience. In less than an hour, they amassed a truly unhealthy quantity of candy.

When it started to get late, they all hugged Tau and he headed home, still wearing his antlers, to show Lusa. And, finally, the Better Angels went back to *Angels' Wings* to get ready for bed. And sweet dreams.

●　　　●　　　●

Almost two months later, David and the Better Angels offered a benefit performance running a Thunder Cross booth at the World Convention on Volpex. There was a throne for him to sit on and he was wearing the white goatee and string tie of Thunder Cross. The Angels were dressed as his elves, managing the line, receiving children to sit on his lap, and conducting the photography.

"*Meri kurisumasu!*" Thunder Cross said, nodding to the children.

The line to meet Thunder Cross went around the entire convention center. Each eager child would be accepted by the elves, passed up to Thunder Cross, and photographed sitting on his lap. Each child was sent away with a picture and a little red-and-white bucket of candy and toys.

"*Meri kurisumasu!*" Thunder Cross said to each child.

•   •   •

Besk awoke in Miss Clit's bed and, in a flash of lightning, saw David standing at the foot of the bed pointing a railgun at him. Miss Clit was already dressed and carrying a bag. David passed her a thick envelope and said, "Go!" Besk heard the door latch as she left.

"You must be the one who got Tove," Besk said, trying to reach surreptitiously for his device. "What do you want to know?"

David shot him in the head.

"Nothing," he said. He went out the door into the rain, tossing a nanobomb behind him.

•   •   •

At the close of the convention, the Angels circled around Thunder Cross and, pulling on his shirt, led him back to *Angels' Wings*. The convention center was connected directly to the spaceport. Outside, they could see the heavy rain coming down.

"*Meri kurisumasu!*" he said to passersby in the corridors of the spaceport.

Once they entered through the hatch of *Angels' Wings*, the Angels led him directly to the massive recycler and pushed him inside.

"*Meri kurisumasu!*" he said as he slid down the chute.

"Bye, bye!" Mumu called after him.

The Angels turned and found the real David, who had entered using the cargo door. He looked baleful, standing alone, drenched and still dripping on the deck. Zaza stepped forward.

"Stand down, David!" she said. "Stand down!"

THE BETTER ANGELS
AND
THE SUPER STICKY SITUATION

DAVID STEPPED INTO THE GALLEY of the *Angels' Wings* and surveyed utter destruction. Everywhere he looked, disaster reigned. The sink was full of dirty pots and pans. The counters were sticky. The floor was stickier. The stove was coated with some dark substance. The oven was standing open and the racks were filthy. There were splashes on the cabinets. And the walls. Even the ceiling was splattered. Everything was a frightful mess. David sighed ...

He was already exhausted. He'd finally returned in the late afternoon in mid-February after being tied up all morning dealing with red tape for an upcoming tour. He'd spent hour after hour visiting offices in the Truck Stop at the Center of the Galaxy: first one office had directed him to another and then to another and another until the ninth sent him back to the first. He hated dealing with people. And this! This was it. This was the end. This was the very last straw.

Seeing red, he stomped out of the galley. He glared out toward the lounge. The Better Angels were sprawled on the couches asleep. He almost yelled, but then he paused, considering. He took a few deep breaths. He needed to be firm. But he mustn't lose his temper. He drew in his breath to say something when Zaza cracked an eye and spotted him.

"Angels! Angels!" she said, excitedly. "David's back!"

"He's back! He's back!" they said, as they yawned, stretched, and leapt to their feet. They assembled in formation before him.

"Angels," he said, firmly. "I just want to say ..."

"Happy Valentine's Day, David!" they shouted all together. Zaza stepped forward and handed him a little bag. Puzzled, he lifted it up and looked inside. There were eight, little, chocolate angels. And one pair of red chocolate lips.

"We each gave you one angel," Zaza explained. "But I gave you the lips. Just from me."

David turned bright red. He looked down for a moment to recover his equanimity, then he looked up and smiled.

"Thank you, Angels," he said. "This ... This may be the nicest thing anyone's ever done for me. I really appreciate it. But, I have to say, when I came back and found the mess in the galley I was pretty upset. And I'm still puzzled how you made such a mess just making eight or nine little chocolates."

"Oh. Well," Zaza said. "Since NeoBoxers can't have chocolate, we also had to make dog biscuits for Tau."

Each Angel held up a bag of heart-shaped dog biscuits.

"C'mon, Angels!" Zaza said. "Let's take them to him now!" They ran out in a gaggle shrieking with excitement.

David stood speechless for several long moments. Then he sighed, put on his apron, and started washing dishes. But every so often, he looked to where he had set the bag of chocolates and smiled.

THE BETTER ANGELS
AND
THE REALLY RAPID RESCUE

A LITTLE PALE-SKINNED BLOND GIRL emerged from the dressing room. She had changed into a pink-and-blue, magical-girl costume with rainbow colored ribbons. David could see she was nervous as she looked around anxiously. He crouched down to get on her level.

"Which Angel would you like to pose with?" he asked, gently. David was the manager of the Better Angels, an idol group of non-human biological androids that had rapidly shot to galactic-wide fame. They looked like teen or pre-teen girls and wore distinctive costumes matching the one the girl was wearing. In addition to live performances, they also staged appearances for their fans to benefit charity.

The little girl pointed shyly.

"With Tutu? You've got it!"

Tutu came forward with a smile, took her hand, and raised it over their heads. The rest of the Better Angels struck a pose all around the two of them while the photographer took pictures in front of a backdrop. The little girl grinned from ear to ear and then suddenly gave Tutu a big hug. All of the Angels crowded around and hugged them both.

When her turn was over there was another girl and another and yet another. And finally, three hours after closing the doors, they took the last photograph and sent the last little girl off with a picture and a smile.

After the benefit appearance, David and the Angels delivered the proceeds to representatives of the charity with one last photo op. Then they struck the banners and displays, packed everything up, turned it over to the porteroids to transport, and headed back to *Angels' Wings,* their starship.

Back on the bridge, David entered their flight plan, checked the energy levels, and then, once cleared, lifted off bound for their permanent berth on the Truck Stop at the Center of the Galaxy.

"We ate all our vegetables," Zaza said, coming onto the bridge as they headed toward the jump point. "Did you get us anything for dessert?"

"Funny you should say that," David said, pulling out a fancy paper bag and walking back to the galley.

"Lollipops!" shrieked half of the Angels.

"Bubblegum!" shrieked the others.

"Sorry, Angels. I got only lollipops this time," David said to shrieks and wails in stereo. "But they're bubblegum-flavored lollipops."

To deafening squeals of excitement, he passed them out as fast as he could. And then, when the Angels were content, he went back to the bridge. He'd seen a message-waiting indicator that was from an address that could only mean very bad news. He sighed, brought up the message, and then entered a very long challenge phrase to decrypt it. The message itself was quite brief.

"David," it read. "I'm sorry to reach out to you after all this time, but I need your help. It's important. Contact me the usual way. Urgently, Charles." David leaned back, considering.

•   •   •

When Zaza awoke in the early morning, *Angels' Wings* had returned to its berth on the Truck Stop. Zaza got up and ran out to the bridge to see David, but he wasn't there. She checked his room, but he wasn't there either. By then the other Angels were waking up, so Zaza helped fix breakfast for everyone and, when it was ready, got the last couple of the Angels up.

"Does anyone know where David went?" she asked. She looked around, but everyone was shaking their heads.

After breakfast, she went out to the bridge and pinged his device, but the ping went unacknowledged. She puzzled a bit, but then went back to the galley.

"Let's go, Angels! We need to practice!"

The largest hold in *Angels' Wings*, Hold One, had been converted to a dance studio. Here, the Better Angels spent the day rehearsing for their upcoming performance. This was to be an intimate performance, organized by a wealthy philanthropist, for elderly PuzzyCure fans who had a long list of very specific demands.

•   •   •

"I don't do that work anymore, Mr. Downsend," David had said to Charles. "I'm done. I've got other responsibilities now."

"It's my daughter, David," Charles said, pleading. "She's been kidnapped! You remember Cherry. You're the only one that can do it. You've got to bring her back."

David did remember Cherry. She'd been just a little girl when he left. He remembered her holding his hand and pulling him into her bedroom to look at her dolls. He sighed and relented — as Charles had known he would.

In the dead of night, he outfitted and armed himself, then slipped out of *Angels' Wings* and headed to another berth in the Docking Ring where Charles had requisitioned a fast courier: A Xerxes Mark XIX. David piloted himself to Grendlehein, an automated mining and manufacturing complex where, according to Charles' intelligence, Cherry was being held by a terrorist organization. Using stealth mode, he crept in meters above the surface and landed just out of sight of the facility.

•   •   •

Two days later, Zaza went out to the bridge in the early morning and saw a flashing indicator showing a recorded message that said,

"For the Angels." She ran back and got the rest of the Angels up and brought them into the bridge, then pushed the button. The recording began to play and David appeared on the screen.

"Hello, Angels," David said. "Two days ago I undertook a mission to help my old employer. If you're seeing this, then I have failed and am probably not coming back. Once this message completes, you'll find that I have given all of you access to all of the spaces and functionality of *Angels' Wings*. Stick together. You'll have to look out for yourselves from now on. I love you all."

The message clicked off and then all of the panels around the bridge powered on and they heard a series of clicks and the sounds of doors opening throughout the ship.

"What does it mean?" Nene asked.

"I think it means that David is in trouble," Zaza said. "And I think we should go get him back."

"But how? Where will we go? What can we do?" the Angels said, looking at one another.

Zaza stamped her foot.

"We are the Better Angels!" she said. "If we were in trouble, David would never give up. And we shouldn't either! Lala! Figure out how to work the replicator. Mumu! Search David's Room. Nene! Check recent communications. Popo! Search Hold Two. Rara! Search Hold Three. Sisi! Search the smaller cargo bays. Look for anything that might help us! And Tutu! Read the owner's manual for *Angels' Wings*."

"What are you going to do?" asked Nene.

"I am going to search David's files," Zaza said. "Let's get to work and report back in a half hour."

Zaza brought up David's files on the console and found that, as in all things, he was meticulously organized. His files included correspondence, receipts, and financial reports. But then she found what she was looking for.

After thirty minutes, the Angels reconvened.

"Lala! What did you find?" Zaza asked.

"I found the documentation for the replicator and I can make it work."

"Please replicate eight of these," she said, sending a file to her station.

"Yes, Zaza."

"Mumu! What did you find?"

"David's belongings are all still there, so I don't think he intended to be gone for long."

"Thank you. Nene?"

"I looked through the recent communications and found an endpoint that messaged David and he made a return call. But I can't tell who that is or where they are."

"That's a good start. Popo?"

"I searched Hold Two, but it was just the signage, banners, and lighting for our shows."

"Hold Three is the same," Rara said. "Except it's the sound equipment, cables, and speakers."

"What did you find, Sisi?"

"The first smaller cargo bay is an armory. It has lots of different kinds of rifles, railguns, and firearms. And other weapons too, like knives and grenades and mines."

"I saw that armory once before," Zaza said.

"The second cargo bay has climbing gear," Sisi continued. "There are lots of ropes and harnesses and stuff."

"That may come in handy," Zaza said. "What did you find Tutu?"

"I found the technical readout for *Angels' Wings* along with David's notes. *Angels' Wings* was originally commissioned as a DR-420 military troop transport. Gaetz bought it surplus and converted it into a freighter, but he didn't do a very good job keeping it up. When David bought her, she needed a lot of work, so he had her fully restored and retrofitted. Now, she's even better than she originally was with bigger, more powerful engines and stronger armor."

"And what did you find, Zaza?" Nene asked.

"Hang on. Lala! Are those ready?"

"Yes, Zaza! Here!" She ran in and handed out a device to each Angel.

"What I found was David's repository of personality modules," Zaza said. "It has all of our modules. But it also appears to have all of his, and a whole lot more. He must have been collecting them for a long time. There are modules for all kinds of things: small arms marksmanship, hand-to-hand combat, silent movement, and more. There are also modules for all of the roles in a strike team."

Zaza made a few quick selections at her console.

"I'm going to install David's modules into my stack. If they work for me, I've set up your devices with modules for you to try as well."

Zaza picked up her device, selected the modules in her stack, and pressed accept.

It was as though her vision became monochromatic. Colors seemed to fade. And all of the happiness in the world was squeezed out of it. She immediately became more aware of her surroundings and started noting potential threats and routes of egress.

"You look scary, Zaza," Mumu said. "Are you okay?"

"Affirmative, Recruit. Jacked up and good to go."

"What?"

Zaza quickly made assignments at the console then fixed the other Angels with her steely gaze.

"Alright, Recruits. Lock and load!"

The Angels used their new devices to accept the personality modules. Zaza watched their expressions change as the programming took effect.

"Ready to move out?"

"Yes, Sarge!" they barked.

"Lala! Mumu! We need kit. Replicate uniforms and tactical webbing."

"Yes, Sarge!"

"Sisi! You're our weapons specialist. Select weapons for us."

Sisi made a gesture like shooting a pistol at Zaza, then turned and did a quick march toward the cargo bays.

"Popo! Rara! You're on KP duty. An army marches on its stomach."

They saluted smartly and headed for the galley.

"Nene! You're on comms. Bring up that endpoint that David last contacted."

"On it, Sarge!"

Nene worked the communications console and, after a brief moment, gestured at Zaza.

"David?" said a hopeful voice at the other end.

"Negatory, Civilian," Zaza said. "This is not David. But we think he's in trouble and are preparing backup."

"I was beginning to worry," he said. "But I was hopeful when I saw the connection. Who am I speaking with?"

"Call me Z," Zaza said.

"Code names? Well, I'm Charles Downsend. I'm transmitting the same package of materials I sent to David." Nene nodded.

"Thank you," Zaza said. "Z out." She made a chopping gesture at her throat and Nene killed the connection. Then she turned to Tutu.

"Now, we've just got to fly this thing."

"Bad news, Sarge. We're not pilots. We've got the programming to fly *Angels' Wings* but, without a licensed pilot, Space Traffic Control won't let us detach."

"That's a problem, Private. Options?"

"We could hire a pilot, Sarge."

"Negatory, Private. We need to keep this intimate. But I think I know who we need. Secure the ship until I return."

"Aye, aye, Sarge!"

•   •   •

Cherry was asleep. David had made two quiet kills with his knife to reach the room the kidnappers were holding her in. He stood for a moment and just looked at her. She had been just a small child when he left, but now she was a comely college co-ed. He slipped quietly up to her bed.

"Ssh!" David hissed, putting his hand over Cherry's mouth. She woke up and struggled. "It's me! It's your Uncle David!"

When she realized who it was, she tapped his arm and he removed his hand from her mouth.

"Thanks, Uncle David!" she whispered. "I knew you'd come!"

"Now we just need to get you out of here," he said, giving her a hand up.

He led her to the door and listened. They slipped through and he began to retrace his steps back toward his ship when a deafening roar reverberated through the cavernous facility. The ground shook under their feet. David checked his device.

"Bad news. They found my ship," he told Cherry. "Mission's changed. Now we just try to stay at large for as long as we can and hope for a miracle."

•　　•　　•

As Zaza headed for the exit, Lala and Mumu handed her a set of black fatigues with tactical harness, so she stripped and pulled on the uniform before leaving. Then she exited *Angels' Wings*, cleared Truck Stop security, and took the elevator up to the Green Sector. She walked briskly spinward until she arrived at the Zoological Sanctuary.

"Zaza!" Lusa said, with surprise. "You look different. And serious. Is something wrong?"

"David is missing and we believe he's in danger. Only this time he's not on station. We need to find a pilot."

"I'm not sure I can help you there," she said.

"I am informed that NeoBoxers hold pilot status. Is that true?"

"Is it?" she said with surprise. She consulted her console. "It is! You're correct. Part of the augmentation they receive automatically grants them pilot status. How did you know that?"

"Sorry, Civilian — that information is need-to-know. I formally request Tau's assignment as pilot of *Angels' Wings* for our rescue mission."

"You'll need to ask him. He's just finishing his rounds."

Tau entered Lusa's office and saw Zaza. He was a massive tawny NeoBoxer with a black face. He took in her uniform and expression and immediately barked.

"That's right," Zaza said. "We need your services again. This time, we need you to pilot for us."

Tau barked sharply.

"Captain? You want to be Captain?" Zaza said. "But we only need a pilot."

Tau barked again, more stridently.

"You'll only pilot for us if you're Captain? Isn't that a bit excessive?" Tau turned his back and sat.

"Can you at least tell me why?"

Tau barked again without looking back.

"I understand you want to protect us from danger, but this mission is inherently dangerous."

Tau looked away.

"I hear you, but do you really understand what you're asking me to do?"

Tau snorted.

"I'm not sure *that* language is called for!" Zaza said, stung.

There was a long silence and neither side showed signs of budging.

"Agreed, Captain," Zaza said finally, snapping to attention. "You are Captain and we will follow your orders while we're on board."

Tau sprang to his feet, licked Lusa's face, then barked and headed for the door, with Zaza close behind.

•　　•　　•

The loudspeaker crackled. "Captain Tau? This is Truck Stop Space Traffic Control. *Angels' Wings* is number one for departure."

Captain Tau barked.

"I copy that," Nene said.

Once they detached from the Truck Stop, Captain Tau showed that he understood the true meaning of haste. David tended to be an extremely conservative pilot, but Tau opened the engines up full making a beeline for the jump point. There was some angry chatter from other ships that they passed, cutting ahead of their turn at jump. They reached the jump point and went to jump at full velocity.

"In the pipe," Nene said. "Five by five."

"Squad! Assemble in Hold One! Rig lines for rappelling," Zaza said over the loudspeaker, then turned to Nene. "You stay here, Private, to maintain communications."

"Understood, Sarge."

Zaza went back to Hold One and found the other six Angels at parade rest. She collected the railgun Sisi had chosen for her, checked the charge, metal, and settings; then she hung it on her webbing, along with two additional charge blocks, and four grenades.

"Let's talk tactics, troops," Zaza said.

•　　•　　•

David and Cherry had reached a dead end. David pushed Cherry behind him, and took up a position just around a corner as the remaining kidnappers closed in. He had picked off several as he fought a careful rearguard action, but there were too many left. He checked the charge on his railgun. It was nearly depleted. It wasn't going to be long now. He loosened his knife in its sheath and prepared to make his last stand.

"We both know how this ends," called the leader of the kidnappers. "With a hail of gunfire. Neither of us wants the girl to be injured. Why don't you both surrender? Or, at least, release the girl."

"Never!" yelled David.

"What are you waiting for?" the leader scoffed. "Do you think an angel will come down and rescue you?"

•　　　•　　　•

Angels' Wings came out of jump and they found themselves barreling at high speed toward the facility, which was situated very close to the jump point to facilitate transshipment. Nene initiated a scan.

"David located. He has custody of the civilian. There are enemy forces closing in. Strap yourselves in, Angels!"

Angels' Wings blasted through the atmosphere like a meteor until just a thousand feet above the facility, then Captain Tau slammed the engines to full. The gravity generator squealed as it was hard pressed to compensate for the high G-forces.

"Hang on, we're in for some chop!" Nene announced over the loudspeaker.

There were a series of sharp bangs as canon fire splashed on their armor. They slowed to a hover just above the roof with the engines howling.

Zaza triggered the cargo hatch and then dropped an XRT-47 mine onto the roof, which fell, detonated, and blasted a jagged hole into the facility.

"Go! Go! Go!" Zaza shouted.

Zaza's squad threw their ropes down and rappelled through the opening. The enemy force had been stunned by the sudden roar and detonation. The Angels picked off two while descending on the ropes and the other kidnappers scattered for cover. One exposed his back to David, who did not hesitate to shoot him from the corner where he'd taken up his last stand.

Zaza heard the whine of David's railgun and could tell the charge was fully expended.

"Catch this, Top!" she yelled. Then she drew back her arm, stood up, and made a textbook long pass while bullets flattened themselves all around her. David reached out and, in one motion, ejected the dead powerblock, snagged the one Zaza had thrown, and slammed it home. The railgun whined as it powered up to a full charge. Then David came out from around the corner and began to shoot kidnappers from behind one after another. Caught in a crossfire, the terrorists didn't stand a chance and were gunned down without mercy. As the gunfire ceased, *Angels' Wings* swept to the side and touched down just outside the facility with the engines still at a roar.

"All present and accounted for, Master Sergeant!" Zaza shouted to David, as the Angels all stood and revealed themselves.

"Well done, Sergeant," David barked. "Lala! Mumu! Popo! Cover the incoming corridor! Rara! Sisi! Tutu! Secure the exit. Zaza! Collect the Civilian. Let's move!"

"Yes, Top!" they shouted.

Zaza ran back to where David had left Cherry, around the corner.

"Let's move out, Civilian," she said.

Cherry followed behind Zaza as they headed back.

"You look familiar," she said. "Haven't I seen you before?"

"Negatory, Civilian," Zaza said, the muzzle of her railgun questing as they came back around the corner.

"No," Cherry said. "I'm sure I've seen you somewhere before. Were you on the telly?"

"Stay sharp, Civilian," Zaza said.

"Tell me who you are!" Cherry pressed.

Zaza pulled a business card out of her pocket and, without looking away as she scanned for threats, passed it wordlessly back to Cherry. She studied it. It was an animated card that showed a troupe of magical-girl idols posing with unicorns, teddy bears, and rainbows: *The Better Angels. Entertainment. Music and Dancing. PuzzyCure.* And someone had penned "Rescues" at the end of the list.

"Ooh! PuzzyCure!" she said. "My dad's a huge fan!"

They reached the exit that Rara, Sisi, and Tutu were holding secure. Looking out, Angels' Wings was sitting with the doors opened, but with the engines still running which created a keening roar and kicked dust up for a hundred meters in every direction. Nene appeared in the hatch with a missile launcher.

"Get on board, Civilian," Zaza ordered. "And strap in."

When directed by David, Lala, Mumu, and Popo pulled back from the corridor while Rara, Sisi, and Tutu kept them covered. Once they were aboard, David directed the rest to pull back.

"Now you get on board, Top," Zaza said.

"Ladies first," he said. He and Zaza glared at one another, then moved back together while Nene kept them covered.

"Get down!" Nene shouted and fired the missile launcher. A man had popped up with a weapon on the roof. Her missile caught the edge of the roof and exploded, driving the man back under cover.

Once David and Zaza were aboard, the pitch of the engines rose to a scream while the cargo doors closed and *Angels' Wings* rose on a tower of smoke and flame. David sprinted for the bridge and ... found the captain's seat occupied.

"What's this, then?" he growled.

Captain Tau barked.

For a moment, David and Tau looked ready to come to blows.

"Captain?!? Of *Angels' Wings*? Who signed off on that?" David snarled.

"I did, Top," Zaza explained, coming up behind. "We needed a pilot and it was his condition to pilot for us."

David brought his temper under control and backed down. He acknowledged Tau with a nod, saying, "Cap'n." Then he took up a position to the right of the Captain and stood with his arms crossed. *Angels' Wings* was still accelerating when she hit the jump point. As they went to jump, Captain Tau let loose in a howl of pure exhilaration. And the Better Angels joined in with perfect harmony.

•   •   •

After flying over miles of beautifully landscaped country estate, *Angels' Wings* touched down on the grass outside the main house at

Kalperion, the Downsend's summer place. Charles was waiting as the engines shut down and the ground-level cargo hatch opened.

"Daddy!" Cherry screamed, running out and throwing herself into Charles' arms.

"Oh, my baby!" Charles sobbed. "I'm so glad you're okay!"

"But you've gotta see this, Daddy!" Cherry said, pressing the business card into his hands. "It's the Better Angels!"

"The Better Angels? You mean the Better Angels we hired to do the PuzzyCure show? Really?"

He looked at the card and his eyes got big, then he looked back toward Angels' Wings and saw David flanked by eight small, heavily-armed soldiers. And one massive NeoBoxer.

"I didn't know this was your outfit now," he said to David, inclining his head. "Ten times your usual fee will be in the usual place. But, going forward, maybe I could put you all on retainer."

Zaza stepped forward and snapped to attention.

"Sorry, Charlie," she growled. "We're David's Better Angels."

With a final salute, they closed the cargo hatch and Captain Tau returned to the bridge, started the engines, and *Angels' Wings* lifted off, bound for the Truck Stop. David and the troop of Angels regarded one another.

"This is the worst part," David said. "Are you ready, Sergeant?"

She nodded curtly and said, "Stand down, David," at the same time that he said, "Stand down, Angels."

They all dropped to the deck as violent spasms shook them. David was first to recover, being more familiar with the effects. He picked up each Angel in turn and carried them to their beds to tuck them in. Zaza had managed to get back on her feet by the time he returned for her. Still trembling, she threw herself on him and hugged him.

"I was so scared, David!"

"I'm sorry, Angel," he said, scooping her up in a princess carry and taking her to her bunk. "Sleep now. And have sweet dreams."

•　　　•　　　•

The next morning, *Angels' Wings* was again berthed at the Truck Stop. Zaza awoke and ran lightly out to the bridge in her nightgown to find David brushing off the captain's seat.

"Everything is covered with dog hair," David grumbled.

After landing, Captain Tau had relinquished the seat and returned to his regular duties.

"Good morning, David," she sang out.

"Good morning, Angel," he said, with a smile.

"It's good to have you back."

"It's good to be back."

There was silence for a moment.

"You must never ever go off by yourself again," Zaza said, putting her little hands on his arm.

He put his hand on hers.

"No, Angel," he promised. "Never again."

•   •   •

The lights dimmed in the intimate theatre and the posh crowd quieted. The first notes of Tchaikovsky's Swan Lake began to play. A murmur arose from the audience as people looked at another, wondering what was happening. Suddenly, a heavy bass cut in with a thumpa-thumpa-thump. Everyone's attention was captured when a bright spotlight illuminated Zaza on the stage, wearing a pink-and-blue magical-girl costume with rainbow ribbons. She spread her arms, bringing up the stage lights. The drums cut in and the rest of the Better Angels began to sing and dance.

David, standing to the side, noted that Charles and Cherry had been seated in the front row. But now everyone was on their feet yelling and screaming with excitement. Charles shouted, "It's PUZZYCURE!"

THE BETTER ANGELS
AND
LAMBDA AND TAU

DAVID RETURNED TO *Angels' Wings* to find Tau surrounded by the Better Angels who were all patting him and rubbing his tummy and telling him, "There, there!" Lying on his back, his muzzle splayed open showing his pink gums and jowls.

"What's with him?" David asked. Zaza grabbed his thumb and led him into the bridge.

She leaned close and whispered, "Right now, there's a girl NeoBoxer visiting the Truck Stop at the Center of the Galaxy."

"Isn't that a good thing?"

"Tau asked her out on a date and got turned down."

"Really? Why?"

"Her boss says they're too busy."

"Huh. She sounds pretty hard core. Oh, well. Those are the breaks sometimes."

"No!" Zaza said, stamping her foot.

"No?"

"That's not good enough. We need to help."

"Ooh. That sounds dangerous. Do you have a plan?"

Zaza rubbed her hands together and whispered in David's ear. His expression, guarded at first, grew mirthful. He grinned. He got out his device and pinged Lusa and Rect.

•　　　•　　　•

Totemo Isogashii was packed and ready to depart. Lambda was sitting next to her in the lobby of the Zoological Sanctuary.

"Thank you for your assistance," she said to Lusa, inclining her head. "You allowed us to finish even more quickly than I had anticipated. But we need to return to Holufinia promptly to put your suggestions into practice."

"I'm glad I could help. I'm sorry you couldn't spend an extra day just to look around and enjoy yourselves."

"We're on a tight schedule," Totemo said. Then her device alerted her. She looked at the screen and her eyes got big. She looked at Lusa. "Is Mx MacFearson who I think it is?"

Lusa's eyes got really big. "That's Bull! She's the CEO of Astro Services. She's Big Time Stuff!"

Totemo held her device up and answered, "*Moshi, moshi*! Yes, ma'am. Yes. Yes, I'll be right there."

She looked down at Lambda.

"Stay! I'll be back in just a few minutes and then we're going."

Lusa walked her to the door as she walked antispinward, toward the Casino. As soon as she turned in, David and the Better Angels hustled into the Zoological Sanctuary. David was carrying a wooden crate. Lulu had a red-and-white table cloth. Mumu had a wine bottle. Nene brought a candle. Popo had a candle holder. Rara had a bowl. Sisi was carrying some breadsticks. Tutu had a big plate. And Zaza was carrying a pot.

They rapidly assembled everything in front of Lambda. The box went on the ground and was covered over with the table cloth. The candle was lit and placed on the table along with the wine bottle and breadsticks. Tutu set the plate down in front of Lambda. And, while she was distracted, Tau slipped quietly in and sat down next to her.

Lambda looked over at him with surprise. The Angels had washed and brushed him so his coat fairly shone. He sat up straight and then looked up at Zaza.

"We weren't sure there was time to order off the menu," she said. "So we took the liberty of just bringing spaghetti and meatballs." She served a generous helping onto the plate.

Then the Angels stood to the side and sang an acapella rendition of *Bella Notte* followed by *That's Amore*.

Lambda and Tau shared the plate of spaghetti. Tau would pick up meatballs, throw them up in the air, and then catch them. Lambda watched and then let her tongue loll out with amusement. When they got to the last meatball, Tau rolled it toward Lambda with his muzzle. She picked it up, bit it in half then tossed both halves up. They both leapt up in the air and each caught one half. Then she licked the sauce off his muzzle.

●　　●　　●

Totemo entered the casino and was met and guided by an administrative assistant to the elevator for a brief ride to the second floor, then down a long, paneled hallway to the club where Bull liked to meet people. Bull was sitting with her back to the door looking out the huge windows. Today, her window was pointed toward one of the nearby jump points where you could see starships coming and going in a steady stream.

"Thank you for coming, Miss Isogashii," Bull said. "I wanted to ask you a few questions about how Holufinia is recovering after ASI completed our work there."

"Our entire planet is very grateful to you, Mx. MacFearson," Totemo said, bowing.

"Please! Call me Bull!" she said, gesturing at a comfortable chair.

●　　●　　●

Tau spun in a few quick circles and then did a play bow, putting his chest and forelimbs flat on the deck. Lambda sat back down and shook her head. Tau charged at her, nudged her with his muzzle, and then sprang back, play bowing again. Lambda pointed at the clock. Tau nudged her with his muzzle again.

"Go on, Miss," Zaza said, encouragingly. "We'll watch the clock for you."

Tau pointed toward the garden in the Sanctuary. Lambda finally couldn't resist and came to her feet. Tau raced back toward the garden, spun, barked, and then raced on. She loped after him. The Angels could hear them barking back and forth as they raced in circles.

Tau led her over to that plant that smelled so weird. He barked and rolled on it. He got up, shook himself off, and snorted. She rolled on it too. Tau's tongue lolled.

•   •   •

"One more question, Miss Isogashii," Bull said, as Totemo got to her feet.

"Alright," she said. "But I'm on a very tight schedule."

"This won't take long," Bull said, tapping her device. "I was hoping you could show our chief engineer which spaceports are currently active on Holufinia. Then he'll walk you back. Rect?"

Rect, who had just come in, in response to his boss's summons, brought in a map and spread it on the table.

"I'm not sure I'm really the right one for this question," she said.

"Just to the best of your knowledge," he said, smiling. "This should only take a few minutes."

•   •   •

Zaza and Sisi looked toward the garden. They saw Lambda and Tau whirling in circles and then abruptly stop, muzzle to muzzle. Tau pointed back behind the stand of bamboo. Lambda, paused and then followed him. Zaza covered Sisi's eyes.

"You're far too young to watch that," she said.

David's device pinged.

"Quick, Angels! She's coming back! Let's clean up!"

•   •   •

"Ah! You're back already!" Lusa said, meeting her at the door to the Zoological Sanctuary. "Did your meeting with Bull go well?"

"Yes!" she said. "I had tried to think of some way to get on her radar while I was here, so it was a real pleasure to have her reach out to me. It made my whole trip doubly worthwhile."

Lusa opened the door and Totemo entered to find Lambda sitting, waiting for her return.

"Let's go, Lambda!"

They walked out of the Sanctuary and headed toward the elevators down to the docking ring. As they went, she noticed a gaggle of young girls wearing short pink-and-blue dresses with rainbow ribbons shrieking with excitement over by McCool's. Lambda pointed and ruffed.

"Really? You're right! That big NeoBoxer is buying ice cream for all those girls. What a good dog!"

THE BETTER ANGELS
AND
THE MONOMANIACAL MENAGERISTE

DARKNESS LAY ON THE CITY. Nene was on her belly positioned on a rooftop overlooking a plaza, peering through binoculars. While returning to the spaceport, after their show on Liggund, the Better Angels had seen a figure who had appeared on a wanted poster, and they turned on their soldier modules in order to apprehend the target.

"Target is moving, Sarge," Nene whispered into the headset.

"Angels hold until target reaches point Zulu," Zaza ordered through her headset.

"Target has stopped. No! He's on the move. Ten meters! Five meters! He's reached point Zulu."

"Go! Go! Go!" Zaza urged.

Six Angels broke cover and charged into the plaza. The target tried to evade them, but Rara was faster.

"Gotcha!" she cried, making the capture. "Come along quietly, Mr. Bubbles," she said to the fluffy white cat in her arms.

David came into the plaza with a pet carrier. Mr. Bubbles saw him coming, made a terrific wrench, and escaped Rara's grasp. But Zaza was there, grabbed him by the scruff, and wrangled him into the carrier.

"You are remanded into custody, Mr. Bubbles," she said.

Ten minutes later, they arrived at Mr. Bubbles' home, where a little girl answered the door.

"Hey, mom! It's the Better Angels. And they've got Mr. Bubbles!"

The Angels, in their black, military fatigues, struck a pose while Zaza passed the carrier over.

"Thank you so much! What do we owe you?" the mother asked.

"No payment is required, Civilian," Zaza said.

"Here! We just finished baking cookies. Please take some!" She brought a tin with cookies for them to carry away with them. They made one more pose for a photo then took their leave.

Afterward, the Better Angels headed to their starship *Angels' Wings*. They spread matts on the floor of Hold One.

"Are you ready Angels?" David asked.

"Yes, Top!" they said, as they stood in formation at parade rest.

"I'm just David, right now," David said. He had not activated his soldier modules.

"Sorry, Civilian," Zaza said. "Force of habit."

"Stand down, Angels," he said. They collapsed to the floor in spasms of trembling. David took a large blanket and spread it over them. Then he went to the bridge and began entering the flight plan to their next engagement at The Ironball while they recovered.

"*Angels' Wings*? This is the tower. You are cleared for departure!"

David locked the console as *Angels' Wings* lifted off in automatic mode. He walked back to the hold where the Angels were starting to get up. He helped them up and sent them to get ready for a late dinner.

"But, cookies!" Popo said, eyeing the tin.

"Not 'til after dinner!" David scolded.

•　　•　　•

Zaza was standing next to David when they emerged from jump. The display showed a fantastic sight where two stars whirled around one another. One was huge and red while the other was small and dark, but with a glowing disk around it, not unlike the accretion disk of the black hole near the Truck Stop at the Center of the Galaxy. But every few seconds the dark star emitted a brilliant flash from above and below the glowing disk. It was mesmerizing as they sometimes synced up and sometimes flashed out of sync, with flashes seeming to bounce back and forth from top to bottom.

"That's amazing, David!" Zaza said, pointing.

"That's Emily," David said. "And the big red star is Clifford. We're headed for The Ironball — that little asteroid there. It's an exclusive resort that's run by an eccentric collector: *La Menageriste*. We've been invited to do a show for a special open house she's holding."

"What does she collect?"

"Unique non-human biological androids."

•   •   •

David piloted *Angels' Wings* into one of the last remaining berths at The Ironball. Once they had come to rest, the Angels started getting ready while David supervised the porteroids that collected the gear for their show. After an hour, they made their appearance.

The hatch hissed as it slid to the side and the Better Angels emerged, in costume. A red carpet had been rolled out and there were velvet ropes. Zaza stepped out first to screams of excitement from crowds lining the ropes. Impassive guards wearing black uniforms were stationed every 5 meters. The rest of the Angels followed, heads held high, as they strutted in formation, smiling and waving to their enthusiastic fans. They stopped periodically to pose for photos or sign autographs. David followed unobtrusively behind, keeping a wary eye on the crowd for threats.

Once they reached the Green Room, they had a while to relax and destress before the show. While the Angels laughed and enjoyed refreshments, David watched a video about the construction of the resort that played on a screen in the room. The entire facility had been constructed inside an M type asteroid. Six giant fusion reactors kept The Ironball in an unstable orbit around the binary star system. Nanobots had removed all of the non-metallic parts leaving only the solid iron core. Then, corridors and rooms were cut into the metal, washed with acid to emphasize the *Widmanstätten* pattern, then coated with a polymer to prevent oxidation. David had to admit, the effect was spectacular. The walls were shiny silver with the striations of the nickel-iron lamellae running crosswise everywhere. The austerity of walls was counterbalanced by recessed lighting, plush carpets, and comfortable furniture. The Angels relaxed in good spirits in advance of their show.

A light flashed high on the wall, a blinking yellow. The Angels, got up and put on their game face. Then the light changed to a steady green and the Better Angels took the stage.

The room was dark with a quiet hubub as the audience anticipated the show. Then a solitary high note bloomed in the darkness, a spotlight lit up Zaza standing by herself, then the rest of the Angels joined in with harmony, singing one of the best known acapella PuzzyCure songs. The audience was spellbound. David watched from the side, still enthralled by the angelic voices of the Better Angels. Then they kicked it up a notch.

The next song had a funky beat and complicated choreography. The Angels moved in perfect synchrony with stylized hand gestures and leg kicks. The audience was enraptured by the performance.

When the first set came to an end, the Angels ended with a characteristic pose, with all of the girls pointing at Zaza who stood at the focus. The audience surged to their feet with thunderous applause.

After the house lights came back up for the intermission, David noticed toward the back, a throne with a slight figure on it watching the performance. She noticed David's gaze and inclined her head in acknowledgment. David returned the gesture, then followed the Better Angels back into the Green Room.

They were in high spirits. They took bottles of water and sank into the luxurious couches and seating provided while they chattered about the show. David stood by the door and kept watch.

David turned in response to a knock at the door. He opened the door and a small man diffidently stepped in.

"*La Menageriste* would speak with the Better Angels," he said. "Would you follow me please?"

He led them through a series of private corridors to an unmarked room and held the door. They stepped through into a museum-like space with rows of large glass display cases. Eight heavily-armed guards stood at attention positioned throughout the room. In the center, was a small girl who appeared to be 12 or 13. She wore a short ruffled black dress, detailed with gray lace, and sparkly black tights. Her blond hair fell in long curls that framed her round face. She had a red fascinator set at a jaunty angle on her head. She offered them a rather predatory smile.

"Welcome to The Ironball!" she proclaimed. "For two hundred years, I have been *La Menageriste*!"

Zaza stepped forward and, in synchrony with the others, curtsied deeply. "We are the Better Angels and we are grateful to you for the invitation to appear at your special open house."

"You are Magicorps girls, are you not?"

"Yes, we have that honor," Zaza replied.

"I thought I had the last Magicorps girl," *La Menageriste* said, waving her hand. A display case behind her had a cloth over it. She swept the cloth away and, inside, they saw a twin to themselves, but with a green collar on her neck and wearing only a sparkly negligee. There was a green leash lying at her feet. She raised her hands to them beseechingly.

A flash of emotion crossed David's face so fast only the most careful observer could have caught it. The corners of the mouth of *La Menageriste* twitched upwards.

"How long has she been here?" David asked.

"Years," she said.

"How do you get her to eat? To drink?"

"I don't," she said. "If I knock her out chemically, I can give her food and water intravenously. And it resets her programming. But if I'm to answer your questions, will you answer mine?"

The Better Angels looked back and forth between David and *La Menageriste* as the tension in the room deepened.

"Keeping her in that state is monstrous and an affront to decency," David said.

"You would be willing to help get her out then?"

"And leave her here as your possession?"

"I only have one: You have eight."

"We are no-one's possession," Zaza said, eyes flashing.

"It's almost time for your second set. Think about it."

•   •   •

The Better Angels took the stage for the second half of the show. The lights dimmed but then there were shouts and a party of four strangely-dressed people appeared around *La Menageriste*.

"Nobody move!" they shouted. "We're from HAMB! That's Humans for the Appropriate Management of Beings. And we're here to liberate all the beings you have imprisoned."

He held up a small device in his hand with a big red button on it.

"We are taking you prisoner. We have planted explosives strategically in The Ironball and, unless you release all of your caged and imprisoned beings, I will scram the reactors and send The Ironball to its doom."

There were shouts of alarm from the audience. *La Menageriste* was unimpressed. She leaned back in her throne and smiled. "But won't that also kill you?"

"That's a price we're willing to pay!"

"And won't it also kill all of these 'beings' you're trying to free?"

"Better death than slavery!"

La Menageriste pressed a button on her throne and her throne dropped down into a shaft and an iron hatch snapped into place over it. The leader of the activists sighed and spoke to the audience.

"I regret that we're going to have to hold you all hostage until *La Menageriste* sees reason. But we will demonstrate that our threats are not idle!"

The moment the strangers had begun to speak, David had pulled out his device and made a few adjustments. His eyes lost their luster and his expression became hard. Zaza watched the changes come over him and realized he had turned on his soldier modules. While the speaker's attention was focused on *La Menageriste*, he had sidled over to the door to the Green Room and cracked the door ajar. While they focused on *La Menageriste*, he quietly called to the Angels.

"This way!" he hissed.

The Angels slipped out of the room in the confusion. David closed and locked the door behind them.

"Follow me to *Angels' Wings*," he ordered.

He led them out the back way. They were running, retracing their steps, when there was a wrenching explosion that caused The Ironball to reverberate. Fissures and cracks began to open in the brittle iron. Gravity winked out for a moment, came back, then winked out again. The lights went out. Sisi, who was last in line, tripped and fell into a crack that had opened in the floor.

•   •   •

When Sisi regained consciousness, gravity had returned, but she was in absolute darkness. She tried opening and closing her eyes and blinking, but could see nothing. She felt for her device, hoping to use it as a flashlight, but it wasn't there. She realized she must have lost it in her tumble.

She felt herself all over and seemed to be mostly uninjured, other than bumps, bruises, and scrapes. There was a small cut on her scalp which had bled quite a bit and the blood had clotted in her hair. She imagined she must look like a terrible fright.

She felt a bit around herself. She was in a rough, unfinished space. It wasn't quite high enough to stand erect. She wasn't sure what to do, her eyes filled with tears, and she was about to cry when she heard something. She strained her ears and realized she was hearing someone singing. It was a PuzzyCure song! She listened for a moment in amazement to hear such pure vocal tones. And what a range! The singer could hit both low and high notes beyond what even Sisi could do. After listening for a few moments, Sisi joined in with the harmony. But then the singing stopped. Sisi held her breath listening, but heard nothing. She was about to cry again when she felt a little puff of breath on her ear.

"Ssso, what are you doing here?" hissed a quiet voice just inches away.

"I'm lost!" Sisi whimpered. "And I've lost my device so I can't see or call for help."

"What'sss your name?" continued the mysterious voice.

"Sisi," she said.

"Sssisssi! What a pretty name!" said the voice.

"What's your name?" Sisi asked.

"Sssindy."

"That's a pretty name too," Sisi said.

"I've found your device," Sssindy said.

"May I have it, please?" Sisi asked, eagerly.

"I'm ssscared," Sssindy said, "that when you sssee me, you'll get afraid."

"I won't be afraid," Sisi promised. "You've been so friendly. And was that your voice earlier? You have such a pretty voice. You must be really pretty too."

"You're ssso sssweet," Sssindy said. "Here you go."

Sisi felt Sssindy press the device into her hands. She turned on the device, which lit up the screen and illuminated the cavern. The light cast harsh shadows from the rough unfinished walls of the iron interior. These were not bright and silvery, but natural and oxidized. But dominating the space was an immense fluorescent pink snake. Sisi could only see part of her, but she must have been nearly 10 meters in length and was as thick around as Sisi herself.

Sisi drew her breath in and then said, in wonder, "Oh, my! You're so BEAUTIFUL!"

"Oh, Sssweety," Sssindy said. "Now, you're makin' me BLUSH!"

"What are you doing down here?"

"It'sss the only place I can hide from *La Menagerissste,*" she whispered.

"Were you a prisoner?"

"You don't know the half of it, Sssweety," she said. "Ssshe inssstalled a persssonality module in my ssstack that letsss her make me do anything. But, down here it doesssn't work."

"What ... What does she make you do?"

"Sssmell things," Sssindy said, and she flicked out a long blue, forked tongue. "I can tell if food is poisssoned. I can also tell when sssomeone isssn't human — Like you Sssweety. Sssometimes ssshe'll make me ssscare people. Or bite them. I don't want to frighten or hurt anyone!"

"Oh, no," Sisi said. "Oh, Sssindy! That's just too sad. And with that beautiful voice too!"

"It'sss missserable down here, but at leassst I'm myssself," she said. "I don't know how I'll ever be able to get away, though."

"Let's ask David," Sisi said. "He was the one who rescued us. If anyone knows how to do it, he will."

"Oh, Sssweety," Sssindy said, sadly. "Now you're makin' me hope. I'm almossst afraid to hope!"

"Can I ... can I give you a hug, Sssindy?"

Sssindy slithered forward and Sisi reached up and hugged her neck. She felt Sssindy's tongue flicker in her ear.

"Don't give up hope!" Sisi said, squeezing her tight. "Don't ever give up hope!"

After they separated, Sisi consulted her device. She found it couldn't connect inside the metallic cavern.

"Can you show me how to get back?" Sisi asked.

"I can point the way," Sssindy said, "but if I go where you can connect, she'd be able to control me."

They went together until Sisi could just detect light up ahead. Then Sssindy hung back while Sisi pressed on. She was scrambling up when David's hand appeared, reached down, and pulled her up.

"David! David!" she started, but he cut her off with a hiss and beckoned to her to follow him back to *Angels' Wings*. Only when the hatch had closed, did he spin and bark, "Report!" at her.

"I fell in a crack and this really nice, uh, girl helped me find my way back," she said, the words just tumbling out. "Her name is Sssindy. She's trying to get away because *La Menageriste* is being mean to her!"

"Girl?" David asked, raising an eyebrow.

"Well ... She's ... She's a girl ... snake. But she's so pretty! And you should hear her voice! She's got a voice like nobody else!"

"Really?" David said. He pondered for a moment and then a really scary smile played across his features for a moment. "That gives me an idea. Mumu! Rara! Sisi! Tutu! Lock and load! Let's give *La Menageriste* a call."

They adjusted their modules, changed into fatigues, and reported back.

"Jacked up and good to go, Top!"

•   •   •

David walked to the bridge and opened a connection. *La Menageriste* came on the screen. She inspected David and showed a satisfied expression.

"Finally. I like you better like this. Much better."

"We will take care of the problem," David said. "But it's going to cost you. And we need Sssindy for the plan to work."

"If you can find her, I will allow her to participate. I'll give you access to her interface."

"Roger and out," David said, cutting the connection. "Sisi! As weapons specialist, choose four sniper rifles for your squad. Stand by, Angels. I must do one thing before we move out ..."

He spent a few minutes at his console. Zaza could see he was looking at a display of a programming interface with Sssindy's name on it. Then he pressed a few keys and a whole list of names appeared, but the only one she recognized was Sssindy.

•　　•　　•

Sisi retraced her steps into the cavern and found Sssindy where she'd left her.

"Sssisssi!" she said. "You came back!" Then she took in Sisi's change in costume and expression. "What'sss happened to you! You look different. And ssscary."

"Sorry, Civilian," Sisi said. "Different programming. We have a plan to rescue you and the others. But we require your assistance."

"Really? What can I do?"

"Do you know *Tears of Shame*?"

"Well, of courssse, Sssweety. Everyone knowsss that one! Tho I can't actually make any tearsss, you know."

"Follow me, Civilian."

•　　•　　•

Sisi led Sssindy to the Green Room. David and the Better Angels were already there. Lala, Nene, Popo, and Zaza were in costume, they ran over and cooed over Sssindy while the others stood by at parade rest cradling sniper rifles. Once they'd returned, Sisi picked up her rifle and joined the others.

"I'm ssso nervousss," Sssindy said, her tail twitching and vibrating on the floor.

"You'll be fine! You'll do great!" The Angels in costume cheered her on.

"Break a leg!" Zaza said with a wink.

Once everyone was ready, Zaza walked boldly out of the Green Room onto the stage. The audience, which had been becoming increasingly restive, quieted for a moment with this new development.

"Who are you? What are you doing?" asked the leader of HAMB, his finger on the button.

"For our featured performance of the night," Zaza said, as if he hadn't said anything, "we present Sssindy Ssserpent singing *Tearsss of Ssshame*."

The spotlight shone down as Sssindy took the stage. There were gasps and some cries of alarm as she slithered out and coiled around one of the microphones. The four Angels stood close by. The house lights dimmed, making Sssindy truly glow. She flicked her long, blue tongue nervously and the audience held their breath.

Sssindy started tapping a beat with her tail on the stage, the Angels provided backing vocals, and she began to sing.

When I can sssee that little gleam
When I can sssee you make that sssmile
You think I'll jussst give up my dream
Becaussse that'sss alwaysss been my ssstyle

The audience, who had been on-edge, exhausted by the stress of the evening's events, began to relax from hearing this old, favorite song. Everyone focused on Sssindy's outstanding beauty and unequaled vocal talent. Even the HAMB activists were captivated.

You need to look me in the eye
You need to give me what I need
'Caussse if you don't I won't jussst cry
I'm gonna cut you till you bleed

The chorus brought the audience out of their seats and many began to sing along. Nobody noticed as the rest of the Better Angels slithered out of the Green Room and made a low crawl through the shadows at the back of the stage, cradling their sniper rifles and taking up positions in the darkness near the edges of the curtains.

You're going to find yoursssself alone
There'sss no one elssse for you to blame
When all your feelingsss turn to ssstone
You're going to drown in tearsss of ssshame

When the final line was being sung, a single report rang out in the auditorium and all of the HAMB activists dropped as one, with neat bullet holes through their foreheads.

Zaza sprang from the stage, sprinted out, and seized the device with the red button before anyone could react. David appeared on the stage and took the microphone.

"Attention Civilians! The reactors have been scrammed and The

Ironball is no longer safe. Please evacuate in an orderly fashion. Return to your ships and depart immediately. Angels assist!"

Screams broke out as people began to surge toward the exits. The Angels headed to the doors and encouraged people to be patient and not shove or crowd one another.

Sssindy looked around in confusion, not sure which way to go or what to do. David approached her.

"Pardon me, Civilian," he said. "It's time for us to depart."

"That sssoundsss nice, but what about *La Menagerissste*?"

David's lips twitched. "Yes, there is one more unpleasant task to accomplish."

David led Sssindy out through the now-empty auditorium and past the dead bodies of the HAMB activists. When they reached the lobby, the Angels were there.

"The guests are away, David," Zaza said.

David extended his hand and Zaza placed the device with the red button in it.

"It's time for us to speak with *La Menageriste*," he said.

•　　　•　　　•

They arrived at the room with the collection of *La Menageriste*. They had to push past her guards that were clustered around the door. She was facing away when they entered, but then she turned and faced them, backed by more guards.

"What have you done!" she snarled, losing her composure completely. "You lied about the reactors!. And you've ruined my open house! Sssindy! Seize him! Bite him!"

Sssindy drew back with a look of horror, then realized she was no longer under the compulsion to obey. She reared up and hissed at *La Menageriste*.

"What? How?" she sputtered.

"I uninstalled that module," David said, advancing on *La Menageriste*.

"Guards! Seize them!" she said, pointing angrily.

While she was speaking, David tapped the screen on his device and her guards all collapsed on the ground, lolling about and sticking their tongues out.

"What's happening? What have you done?"

"I simply gave them all of Sssindy's modules," David said. "You should remember to apply security patches more frequently."

"Oh! You're dead," she said, drawing herself up. "I will track you to the end of the galaxy. There won't be a system small enough for you to hide in."

David sprang forward. He grabbed her head and, before she could react, he broke her neck with a quick twist. He dropped her corpse like a broken doll. Then he stepped to the display case that contained the Magicorps girl, who was still gesticulating and begging. He opened the case, picked up the leash, and snapped it onto her collar. She began jumping for joy and clung to David's arm.

"Angels! Release and conduct the rest of the prisoners to *Angels' Wings*," he ordered. Then he pressed the red button and tossed the device over his shoulder. Klaxons sounded as he walked briskly out. The floor began to shake and the gravity felt unstable as they hustled to their starship.

They boarded *Angels' Wings* with Hold One jammed with dozens of various odd and unusual non-human androids, many obviously designed for highly specialized purposes. They were happy to be rescued from the clutches of *La Menageriste*, but disoriented and confused. Sssindy looked scared and lost, until Sisi found her and said, "Stay close to me, Civilian."

"Thanksss, Sssweety!"

David handed the leash for the Magicorps girl to Zaza and walked to the bridge. In moments, he had disengaged from The Ironball and they stood off. As *Angels' Wings* turned and headed toward the jump point they watched through a display as The Ironball spiraled down, down, down toward Emily — the white dwarf — and was consumed.

"Mumu! Replicate this!" David ordered, sending her a file.

"Yes, Top!"

He locked the console and walked back.

"Let me go! Let me go!" the Magicorps girl said, struggling to pull off her negligee. David pulled out his device and, using the low-level troupe-synchronization code, he deleted Gaetz's crude Little Angel module. The girl suddenly looked around in terror and tried to cover her nakedness.

"Please, Mr. Producer!" she begged, tears in her eyes. "Please, can't I have some real clothes?"

David gestured and Mumu passed the outfit she had replicated for her.

"Oh, Mr. Producer! How did you know?" she squealed, excitedly pulling them on. "A magical PuzzyCure dress and tights! Thank you! Thank you, Mr. Producer!"

"I am David," he said. "What should I call you?"

She cocked her head over, thinking.

"I don't remember my name, David," she said. "Can you give me one, please?"

"Your name is Bebe," David said. She nodded enthusiastically and whispered it to herself.

"Get her something to eat, Angels," David said. "She would probably like a ..."

"A Fun Meal," Tutu said. "On it, Top."

"See what the others in Hold One would like too," he said, as he headed to the bridge.

"Yes, Top!" said four Angels at the same time as the other four said, "Yes, David!"

Once they had gone to jump and everyone was taken care of, David ordered the four Angels to stand down. They collapsed with the shakes. The other Angels caught them and helped them to bed. Sssindy was horrified.

"What'sss wrong with Sssisssi?" she said in a panic, her tail vibrating with tension.

"This just happens when we turn off the programming," Zaza said. "Don't worry. She'll be okay in a little while."

Sssindy looked sad and frightened and would have cried if she were able.

Sisi opened her eyes and reached a hand out. "C-c-can Sssindy s-s-sleep with m-m-me?" Sssindy slithered into her room and coiled up in a corner, but she let Sisi pull her tail into bed with her and clutch it to her while she recovered.

Zaza closed the door then turned.

"Your turn, David."

He nodded and laid down in his bed.

"Stand down, David," Zaza said, gently. Then, as he shook uncontrollably, she tucked him in and closed his door.

•　　•　　•

The next morning, Zaza ran out to the bridge in her nightgown. David was already there, watching the countdown until the end of jump. They smiled at one another in companionable silence.

David watched the newsfeed as they approached the Truck Stop at the Center of the Galaxy. The coverage was dominated by news that activists of the Humans for Appropriate Management of Beings (HAMB) had caused The Ironball to be lost with unknown casualties. Little was known, it was reported, as the entire facility had been destroyed, so there was no evidence regarding the catastrophic events. David and Zaza grinned at each other.

Once they were settled into their berth at the Truck Stop, the Angels made a gauntlet and said goodbye to those rescued from the collection of *La Menageriste*. David had messaged ahead and a number of services had sent representatives to help the newcomers get settled with temporary housing and employment.

"Bye, bye! Bye, bye!" the Angels said, waving. Bebe was in with everyone and ecstatic to be part of the group.

"Well, Sssweety," Sssindy said to Sisi. "I guesss thisss isss goodbye."

"No!" Sisi said, running over and hugging Sssindy. "I don't want you to go! Can't you come tour with us? At least for a while?"

"What do you think, David?" Zaza asked.

The other Angels all chimed in. "Yes! It's okay, isn't it, David? She can come with us can't she?"

"Sssindy Ssserpent and the Better Angelsss?" David said. "It does have a nice ring to it."

"Yay!" they all squealed, hugging Sssindy. She coiled around them all and gave them a big squeeze.

THE BETTER ANGELS
AND
THE REPUGNANT RAMPANT RUMOR

AFTER A SHORT DELAY, David arrived at the hatch of *Angels' Wings* and opened it after someone buzzed. A young man dressed in business casual stood in the spaceway connecting them to the docking ring of the Truck Stop at the Center of the Galaxy. He grinned when the hatch opened.

"Hoo!" he said. "Finally! My messages have evidently not been getting through."

"What do you want?" David said, looking down. He didn't like dealing with people, as a rule.

"Straight to the point! I like that!" the man said, excitedly. "We're from CBMISonVeriNetfrimechyronaMAX. We want to produce a themed, animated show about the Better Angels! By day, they sing and dance. But at *night*, they become the *Avenging Angels* and ... Wait! What are you doing?"

David had placed his hand on the man's chest and pushed him back then he closed the hatch in his face. David rubbed his hands briskly and walked back to the bridge, dodging the Angels, who were playing catch with plushies, cautiously stepping over Sssindy's tail, that was vibrating with tension over all the excitement, and being careful to not kick the bunnies, because there were, in fact, a dozen or more rabbits hopping around. Nobody was quite sure how many. It was just another day aboard *Angels' Wings*.

"Bebe has it!" Bebe shrieked backpedaling. David crouched down and caught her when she ran into him, then he caught the plushie and handed it to her.

"Thanks, David!" she squealed, then she stood up and threw it as hard as she could while the other Angels laughed and shrieked with excitement. David smiled and stepped into the bridge.

They were preparing for a weekend musical performance and military operation. David went down his checklist. Check! Check! Check! They were just waiting on one thing. Or rather one NeoBoxer. David heard the hatch trigger.

"Cap'n Tau!" the Angels shrieked. "It's Cap'n Tau!" Sssindy's tail beat a tattoo on the deck.

David heard his nails click on the deck as he did the same dance David had just done to reach the bridge. David stood and relinquished the captain's chair. Tau hopped up, tongue lolling.

"Cap'n," David said, acknowledging him. "Thanks for coming on short notice. We can really use you on this one."

"Captain Tau?" the speaker crackled. "Truck Stop Space Traffic Control. You're cleared for departure."

Captain Tau barked.

"We copy that," David said.

This time, Captain Tau laid in a relaxed course to the jump point. They heard shrieking and then a plushie flew into the bridge and David snatched it out of the air just before it struck Captain Tau. He looked at Captain Tau, grinned, and handed the plushie to him, then they both headed back to join the fray.

•　　•　　•

The next afternoon, the Angels were offering a benefit concert under sunny skies in a town park. They had a lively crowd, though small. The town wasn't really big enough to purchase a concert, but they had won a contest to bring the Better Angels to perform. The townsfolk didn't need to know that their performance was actually the cover for a covert military operation.

While the Better Angels performed in the park, David observed from a nearby rooftop. The music of their voices carried and made David smile. Then a flock of pigeons flew up, disturbed by an air scooter crossing the plaza. David had chosen his vantage point carefully. He watched the air scooter skirt the edge of the park then leave town and take the winding road toward the hilltop. Eventually, he saw the gate of the hilltop castle open to admit the scooter.

"*Got 'em!*" David thought.

David contacted Captain Tau.

"We are go, Cap'n," David said. "I will move to point Delta. Prepare for Operation Angel Drop."

Tau barked affirmatively and cut the connection.

David also skirted the park as he headed toward the castle. He caught Zaza's eye and waved to her and indicated where he was going. She waved back.

Two men walking past the park were talking as they passed David. David missed what they said at first, but overheard one say, "But by night, it's said they become the *Avenging Angels* and ..." David advertently stuck a foot out and may have tripped the man.

•　　•　　•

Angels' Wings lifted off on schedule, but then diverged from their flight path. The tower contacted them, asking about their situation.

"We copy that," Nene said, acting as communications officer. "We have a stuck hatch, Tower. We're going to hold in a pattern until we can get it locked down. *Angels' Wings* out!"

"Bebe is scared," Bebe said, holding her device. The other Angels had all activated their soldier modules, but Bebe had never done it before.

"Lock and load, Recruit," Zaza said. Then put a hand on her shoulder. "You'll do just fine, Soldier." She watched as Bebe accepted the additional modules. Her eyes widened and then narrowed.

"Bebe is jacked up and good to go, Sarge!" she said.

In the back, Angels made their final preparations and then triggered the cargo hatch. The air swirled around them and the roar of the engines trebled in volume.

"Let's move!" Zaza said and took a running leap out the cargo door, followed closely by the seven others. They tumbled for a moment until they were clear of *Angels' Wings* slipstream and then they unfolded their arms and legs and their wingsuits caught the quiet, evening air.

They flew in a tight formation. They had clear skies with stars overhead and lights laid out in neat rows along streets below. They had practiced using their low-level troupe synchronization code to stay in perfect formation as they sailed down.

Streaking in from the south, under cover of darkness, they dove on the hilltop castle. Once they cleared the wall, they triggered their 'chutes and dropped into the bailey of the castle. Zaza touched down and began quietly rolling up her parachute. Then she helped Bebe who came in last and had the least experience.

Once they'd tucked their 'chutes out of sight, they moved toward point Delta. There were three guards keeping watch at the entrance. Zaza silently gestured to give directions to her troops. The guards at the left and right were hit with garrotes from behind by Lulu and Mumu. Zaza did a spinning kick attack and struck the last in his throat. He dropped, strangling, and Bebe kicked him in the head, knocking him out cold. Popo and Rara tied into the alarm wiring. Sisi and Tutu kept watch.

Once the alarm was disabled, they quietly opened the gate. David, who was standing close at hand, trotted in and passed out railguns to four Angels and missile launchers to the others.

"We gotta move!" David hissed. "We're fourteen seconds behind schedule."

They entered the keep of the castle and mounted the stairs. David led them to a door, opened it quietly, and slipped inside with Zaza. They were in a darkened bedroom with a large, four-poster bed with curtains draped.

"Professor Thombert?" David whispered.

"Huh? What?" a high, squeaky voice said behind the drapes.

"We're here to retrieve you, Civilian," David said, ambiguously.

"Hang on. One moment!" the voice went on, as David began to pull back the curtains around the bed. "Are you familiar with my current ... state?"

"I have not the least idea, Civilian," said David, yanking back the drapes.

In the bed was a rabbit. Then the rabbit spoke.

"Although I may appear to be a rabbit to your uneducated eyes, I am actually a smeerp."

"A smeerp?"

"Yes," the smeerp said. "I am Professor Thombert."

"Did you say 'Thumper'?" David asked.

"No! Thombert! It's pronounced tomb-BEAR!"

Zaza grabbed him, saying, "Let's move, Thumper!"

They slipped back out the door. Sisi had stayed by the door and directed them to Rara who was standing by a stairway. They headed that way with Sisi taking the rearguard. They climbed up, picking up another Angel at the top. They crouched as they crossed a short section of open wall and met another Angel, then they entered a guard tower over the entrance they had come in where the rest were waiting. Inside, they climbed a stairway until they reached a trapdoor.

"Go for Operation Touchdown!" David whispered into his headset. Captain Tau barked affirmatively as Nene calmly said, "We copy that."

David threw back the trap door and the Angels sprang out. The four with missile launchers sighted the anti-aircraft emplacements on the other towers of the castle. They fired the missiles within milliseconds of one another and the four emplacements were blown into the air. David threw the trapdoor back down and wedged it. Then he pulled out his railgun and began looking for targets of opportunity. He fired several times as he saw heads poke out of windows and doors.

Moments later, with a terrific roar, *Angels' Wings* descended to the top of the guard tower. Everyone piled in the open cargo hatch. David sprinted for the bridge. Professor Thombert took this moment to kick Zaza hard. He tried to spring back out the hatch when a long, pink neck snaked out, snatched him out the air, and swallowed him whole.

"Pardon me, Civilian," Sisi said, patting her friend Sssindy, who was a 10-meter long, thicc, pink snake. "That's the scientist. Please don't eat the scientist."

"Oh, my goodness!" Sssindy said, disgorging Professor Thombert. "I was just makin' sure the bunnies don't get away!" He laid on the deck sodden and just twitched for a moment or two, then he suddenly drew in a breath.

"Let's wash you off, Thumper," Zaza said, directing him to a bathroom.

"It's Thombert," he muttered, trying and failing to maintain some modicum of dignity.

•   •   •

David arrived on the bridge as *Angels' Wings* lifted off from the guard tower.

"We've got company, Cap'n," Nene said. "Air fighters. Twenty klicks out and closing."

Captain Tau barked and opened the throttle wide. Once they cleared 500 meters, however, klaxons went off and a red light began flashing.

"That's a targeting scan!" David said. "Dive!"

Angels' Wings dove for the deck.

"Fighters coming on, heading oh-nine-four," Nene said, calmly.

"Heading two-six-six," David said, "Speed, mach two point four."

Angels' Wings flashed over the countryside waking people for miles around with a deafening sonic boom, followed a second later by the booms caused by the pursuit aircraft.

A klaxon sounded.

"A missile that launched when we briefly showed ourselves has locked on," Nene said, her voice an island of calm among the alarms and klaxons.

Tau barked.

David looked up and laughed, "An Ivan! Ha! You're the crazy one!"

With no further warning, *Angels' Wings* flipped around and was pointed the other direction, engines still redlined. Captain Tau howled and the gravity generator joined in. The missile flashed past and reversed direction. The two fighter aircraft tried to turn, but clipped each other and got tangled up. Spinning, they couldn't maneuver when the missile returned and locked onto them. As they exploded over the ocean, Tau took *Angels' Wings* straight up and headed for the jump point at full throttle.

"Now that was amazing piloting! Gimme five! I mean four! Gimme four!" David said, extending a hand. Captain Tau snorted, but then put a paw in his hand. As he laid in the new course to the jump point David walked back from the bridge.

"Angels, report!" he said.

"All secure, Top!" Zaza said.

"Where's Thumper?" David asked.

"There was a minor mishap and the Professor was … well … eaten," Zaza said.

"Eaten?" David said, raising one eyebrow.

"Sssindy mistook him for one of her feeder rabbits," Zaza clarified. "But she spat him up and I helped him to bathe." It was much easier to speak with the Angels about the true nature of the resident rabbit population while they were using their soldier modules – it was a fact they tended to reject otherwise.

"Where is he now?"

"We're not sure, Top. We think he's refusing to talk, hoping to blend in with the rabbits.

"It sounds like Thumper's figured out that we know he wasn't being held by the paramilitary organization but was, rather, a ringleader."

"I believe that's safe to assume, Top."

"Well, Sssindy can pick him out whenever we want," David said. Then he tousled Bebe's head. "How did Bebe do her first time out."

"Commendable!" Zaza said.

"Give Bebe something to shoot!" Bebe said, pumping her fist.

•　　•　　•

Arriving at planet Yarmoth, *Angels' Wings* was directed to land near the venue for their next show, a huge stadium. They had marked off an area in a nearby field and had rolled out the red carpet for them.

"It feels weird to go out there dressed like this, Top," Zaza said, trying to pull her PuzzyCure magical-girl dress farther down. "This uniform is awfully ... breezy."

"You can do it, Sergeant!" David said. "This is where they're most likely to try to hit us. We need to go out there ready for action."

"Yes, Top."

The hatch opened and the Better Angels emerged. They heard a bell tolling six as they began to stalk down the red carpet. Cheers turned to puzzlement as people took in their grim expressions and rolling gait as they marched in formation down the aisle.

"Strike a pose," David hissed.

The Better Angels pantomimed aiming rifles, targeting the audience, and throwing grenades. There were gasps.

"*Avenging Angels*," people whispered. "They're the *Avenging Angels!*"

"Freeze," someone called. Emerging from the audience was a team of eight armed men in military fatigues. "Release the Professor or the girls get it."

There was a frozen tableau as everything stopped. During the silence, a small furry form appeared at the hatch.

"I will be taking my leave now," Professor Thombert said. "And, for your information, it's pronounced tomb-BEAR!" He hopped over the threshold and was suddenly yanked back by a huge pink snake that appeared, snatched him out of the air, and gulped him down. Again.

The armed men were distracted for a fraction of a second and the Better Angels struck. Leaping up in whirling kick attacks, they took down seven of the men with savage kicks to the throat. The last managed to block the kick, but not Bebe's stiffened fingers that struck him in the eyes.

With a roar, a cry went up from the crowd, "*Avenging Angels!* HELP THE ANGELS!" The crowd advanced on the armed men, lying helpless on the ground and began to kick and stomp them. Guards eventually reached the men and took them into custody, but not before they'd been beaten black and blue.

There was mass confusion with screams and pandaemonium until Captain Tau came out with a limp-and-slimy Professor Thombert clamped in his jaws. He passed him over to the guards and then established order, bringing the unruly crowd back under control.

David and the Angels pulled back to *Angels' Wings*. With the situation now under control, they went into Hold One, pulled out the matts, and told each other to stand down. Under Sssindy's watchful eye, they took the time necessary to recover from the spasms of trembling that always followed turning off the soldier modules.

"Bebe d-d-doesn't l-l-like this," Bebe whimpered.

Sssindy laid her tail where Bebe could hug it to her. "Awww, Ssssweety. It'sss a little ssscary," she said. "But you'll be jussst fine in jussst a few minutesss."

One hour later, they all emerged once more to the cheers of the crowd. And, this time, Sssindy went with them.

"We made the arrangements for this performance before you joined us, so I'm sorry you're still not getting top billing," David apologized.

"I don't mind," she said, her tail vibrating nervously. "I'm happy jussst being a guessst performer, for now."

Smiling and waving, Sssindy and the Angels accepted the adulation of their fans as they made their way to the stadium. They stopped frequently to pose with fans and sign autographs. Sssindy had been practicing holding a pen with her tail.

"What a beautiful signature!" a fan enthused when Sssindy signed a program for her. "I love how the Y is like your tongue!" Sssindy had developed a cute signature with the S looping under her name to the Y. Sssindy was still so nervous in public, that her signature was often a bit shaky.

When they reached the building, the music had already started. Fans sprinted for their seats while Sssindy and the Better Angelsss headed straight for the stage.

Performing a series of backflips down the middle aisle, the Better Angels formed a gauntlet with waving hands as Sssindy slithered between up the stairs and into the spotlight. As she coiled around a microphone, the Better Angels struck a pose and the band went silent. Everyone held their breath as Sssindy tapped her tail on the stage to start the beat and they moved seamlessly into their first number.

THE BETTER ANGELS
AND
THE NIGHTY-NIGHT NURSES

S SSINDY AND THE BETTER ANGELSSS arrived at the Windsor Downsend Memorial Children's Hospital in the pre-dawn hours. A courier service had whisked them from the Starport under cover of darkness to prevent hordes of paparazzi or fans from mobbing the hospital. They hustled or slithered, accordingly, through a loading dock entrance and took a service elevator up to the first floor. David stayed circumspectly in the background as they emerged into a ward filled with children who shrieked with excitement to see their favorite idols.

While medicoids bustled back and forth, the Better Angels struck a pose all pointing at Sssindy who reared up and began to belt out the PuzzyCure Morning Song.

When the sssun comesss up,
it'sss a ssspecial sssign ...
The birdsss all sssing in the
more teru pine ...
Wake up! Wake up!
It'sss time to ssshine!

The Better Angels danced and provided backing vocals while the kids joined in and, the ones who could, danced along and did the familiar hand motions. When the song came to a conclusion, everyone turned around three times, like usual. Then they all laughed and cheered and clapped while the Angels took a bow.

Afterward, Sssindy and the Angels fanned out and visited the children who were too sick to come out to the common room in the ward. The children, sick as they were, were cheered to see the Better Angels and some tried to get up. The Angels approached bedsides and held the children's hands and, with gentle smiles exhorted the children to get better soon.

After the first ward, they visited another and another. By early afternoon, they had reached the Gender Affirming Clinic when a sudden explosion rocked the building and the power went out. Power came back on, as backup generators kicked in, when there was another explosion and the power went off altogether. Harsh emergency lights snapped on, powered by local batteries.

"What's happening, David?" Zaza asked.

"I'm not sure. I'm going to try to get to *Angels' Wings* and bring it closer. It might be possible to power the building with our reactor. And I'll try to get information. Watch out, Angels. It may be some kind of attack."

"An attack? What kind of monster would attack a children's hospital?" Zaza said with utter horror.

"There are still superstitious fanatics, like the Hodfollowers, who believe that some medical practices are an affront to their imagined deity," David said. "Fanatics can be dangerous, so be ready for anything, Angels."

"But what about the sick children?" Sssindy asked. "With the power out, the medicoids have all stopped!"

"Watch your devices, Angels. I have some old combat nursing modules that I'll make available once I get to *Angels' Wings*."

With that, David made some adjustments on his own device and they watched as his expression became grim and hard. Then, with a feral lunge, he sprinted out the door and began to run for the stairway down to the parking level.

No sooner had he left, but the Angels heard loud voices and footsteps coming toward Ward A of the Gender Affirming Clinic. There was loud laughter and harsh voices.

"Hod will lead us to the freaks of nature!" one loud voice called. "That we may strike them down!"

"They *are* Hodfollowers!" Zaza whispered. "Angels! Turn on your soldier modules. If they're here for a fight, let's give it to them."

"What ssshould I do?" Sssindy hissed, her tail nervously beating a tattoo on the floor.

"You'll know when the time comes," Sisi said, patting her comfortingly, until she too turned on the soldier modules and her face grew hard and pitiless. Sssindy slithered back out of sight.

The Angels concealed themselves just inside the entrance to Ward A and waited as four men came forward. They slammed through the double doors and marched into the ward, three carrying railguns. One was wearing a backpack and spoke into a device.

"Team Weasel is in position, praise Hod. We'll place the explosives and pull back."

"Copy," said a voice from the device. "I will report your progress to the Hodfather. Teams Fisher and Stoat have checked in, but have not yet reached their positions. Still no word from Team Ermine, Hod protect them."

"Roger that."

Once he put the device in his pocket, Zaza screamed, "Go! Go! Go!" and the Angels launched themselves at the intruders. Each man was confronted with two Angels, one who hit them high while the other hit them low. In moments, the men were incapacitated, strangling and rolling on the floor clutching their genitals. The one with the device tried to press something, but Bebe snatched it away.

"Bebe will take that," she said, handing it to Zaza, who tucked it into a pocket.

The Angels used medical tape to secure the men's hands behind their backs, shoved them in a supply closet, and wedged the door shut. Then Sisi, Tutu, and Zaza took the rail guns.

"Orders, Sarge?" Sisi said, looking at Zaza.

"Let's divide into three strike teams," she said. "Sisi, you take Lala and Mumu and go to Ward B. Tutu, you take Nene and Popo and go to Ward C. I will take Rara and Bebe to Ward D. Let's move!"

Then Zaza turned to Sssindy.

"You stay here, Civilian, and keep watch."

"Yesss, sssir!" Sssindy said.

Zaza grimaced and bit back a comment about not being an officer. But turned and led her strike team down the hall toward Ward D. She checked the settings on the mini railgun. It was set for max velocity and hard slugs, which were enough to blow a giant hole in someone — or pass through multiple interior walls. She turned the velocity way down and set the slugs to be soft, so they wouldn't exit bodies or go through walls.

After the Angels left, the children came cautiously out of their rooms, some crying.

"I'm scared, Sssindy!" one little girl said.

"Don't be afraid," she said, trying to suppress the vibration of her tail. "Grab your blanketsss and let'sss all get together in the lounge and make a pillow fort. That will keep usss sssafe!"

The kids looked unconvinced, but within a few minutes, they were happily building the fort with cushions from the sofas and chairs and peeking out. After a few minutes, there were the typical shrieks of excitement you expect with children at play. Sssindy positioned herself by the door to keep watch. One little boy, who was standing off to the side, approached Sssindy.

"Will you protect us if the bad men come?" he asked.

Sssindy reared up to her full height and said, with as much courage as she could muster, "They'll have to go through me firssst!"

At that moment, they heard the door to Ward A swing open. Sssindy's tail began to vibrate. They heard footsteps and voices approaching.

"Weasel came here, but lost contact. So, as usual, Mongoose has to take up the slack."

"Keep out of sssight!" she hissed at the children, who burrowed into the pillow fort. She flattened herself against the wall beside the door and tried, as best she could, to stop the urge to vibrate her tail.

The men peered into the lounge and saw the pillow fort.

"Check that out!" a heavy-set bearded man said. "What have the little freaks been doing, by Hod?".

He pushed the door open, his railgun hanging at his side, and three men stepped into the room.

"Watch me light 'em up," the man chuckled, pulling up his railgun and thumbing the charge. The railgun whined as he brought it up to aim.

Sssindy silently attacked. She reared up behind them, erected her massive fangs, and struck the man with the railgun, injecting a huge load of venom. His eyes rolled back in his head and he dropped the railgun as he fell to the floor, foaming at the mouth and convulsing violently. She lashed out with her tail, striking the second man in the back. With a horrible crunch, he flew across the room, struck the wall, and fell bonelessly to the floor. The last man froze to see the furious, gigantic, fluorescent pink snake coming at him. She threw a coil around his body and began to constrict. He tried to reach for a knife, but couldn't get his arm past her muscular body that tightened each time he exhaled. Within moments, he was unconscious. And she didn't stop constricting until his heart began to fibrillate and then ceased to beat altogether.

"And ssstay down!" Sssindy hissed at them.

The kids poured out of their fort and cheered Sssindy. "You saved us! Sssindy's the greatest!"

"Oh, ssstop!" she said, turning shyly away. "Now, you're makin' me blusssh!"

•　　　•　　　•

When David left the Angels, the power had been off for three minutes. He sprinted down flight after flight of stairs, until he reached the parking level. He ran through the parking deck until he found the executive parking area and spotted a *Makasete* SpeedRunner, obviously the pride and joy of one of the top administrators. It was black with a custom paint job showing flames and smoke along the sides. It had a soft top that yielded to his fingers until he found the manual release and folded it back. Then he hopped into the plush leather seats and pushed the start button. It rose silently until it was a meter off the ground. He backed it out carefully, then floored it. The power had been off for 8 minutes.

He smashed through the exit gate and turned onto the main thoroughfare. At maximum speed, he zipped in and out among the lumbering ground vehicles, his hair blowing around his face, headed for the spaceport. A police drone took up pursuit and an all-points-bulletin was promptly issued for the hospital administrator.

As David approached the perimeter fence around the Spaceport, he accelerated and then triggered the jump on the SpeedRunner. They were not designed for full flight, but could jump over low obstacles. By jumping up over the cars in a parking lot, and then over a truck that was near the fence, he was able to clear the fence and, setting off alarms all over the spaceport, he sped toward *Angels' Wings* as fast as the SpeedRunner could go.

He abandoned the SpeedRunner and entered *Angels' Wings* through the cargo entrance. He sprinted to the bridge and triggered the explosive bolts on the spaceway. He started the engines and with klaxons and alarms screaming, he blasted off and roared toward the hospital. The power had been off for 14 minutes.

In the three minutes it took to return to the hospital, he consulted aerial photos and identified where the emergency generators were located. Then he went through his archive of programming modules and selected a combat engineer module and installed it in his stack. He made the combat nursing modules available to the Angels via their devices. Finally, he looked up a part number, ran to the giant replicator in *Angels' Wings*, and entered it, to begin replicating a heavy-duty auxiliary power cable.

He made an emergency descent in *Angels' Wings*, with warn-aways wailing constantly, into an alley that ran alongside the back-up generators with only meters to spare on either side. Stopping at the Armory on the way to the cargo hatch, he grabbed a Corona-14 plasma rifle and slung it over his shoulder. Then he dragged the cable out through the cargo hatch, attached it to the external power socket on *Angels' Wings* and dragged the other end toward the building. He saw where the attackers had blown the connection between the emergency generators and the building. At the building, the junction box was housed in a shielded enclosure with a heavy lock. David pulled out the Corona-14 and blasted the lock into molten fragments. Then he removed the cable that had led to the generators, attached the cable from *Angels' Wings*, and sprinted back. Finally, he threw the switch to activate the connection. And nineteen minutes and 40 seconds after the power went off, emergency power kicked in and the Windsor Downsend Memorial Children's Hospital started to come back online.

•   •   •

Zaza led her strike team at a run toward Ward D, through the darkened hallways of the hospital, past immobilized medicoids. As they approached, they heard voices and pressed themselves into the shadows along the walls.

"Hod willing, we need to hit the structural support element just beyond the back wall of this closet that's coming up," a tall, thin man said, consulting a map. "When the bombs go off, they'll cause the building to pancake and crush these abominations."

"Lead the way and I'll set the charges," the third man said.

Zaza realized that they had already passed the closet. Using hand-gestures, she gave directions to Rara and Bebe and they faded back toward the closet and concealed themselves inside.

Rara and Bebe hid on either side of the door behind hospital smocks that hung up on one side and a janitor cart on the other. Once the three men were entirely in the room, Zaza sprang out and shot the leader in the head with the railgun. He toppled over backward with a look of surprise on his face. The other two tried to backpedal out of the room, but Rara and Bebe had moved behind them on their hands and knees, and the men tripped and fell over backward. Zaza sprang forward and shoved the railgun in their faces. Rara collected the railgun the thin man had been carrying.

"I have some questions, Prisoner," Zaza said. "Where are your commanders located?"

"I ain't tellin' you nothin'!" the man with the explosives said. "Hod will protect me!"

Bebe approached with a syringe she had taken from the supply closet. She held it up, tapped it gently, and pressed the plunger, causing a tiny squirt of liquid to spurt up. The man paled.

"What's in that?"

"It is a poison that causes excruciating pain. And then you die," Zaza said. "Talk quickly or she will inject it."

The other man suddenly tried to roll over and grab Zaza's ankle. Without looking, she shot him in the forehead with the railgun. His body went rigid for a moment and then, after a series of tics and twitches, became limp.

"Speak quickly!" Zaza snapped. Bebe advanced on the man with a predatory smile.

"Bebe will take good care of you!"

"They're at the North entrance!" the man said, paling. "Now stop her! She's going to kill me!"

"Negatory," Zaza stated, and shot him in the head.

Bebe tossed the syringe of saline into the sharps disposal.

Zaza was reaching for her device when lights came on in the room and up and down the hallway. It was dim, however, and they realized that only every other fixture was working. They could hear devices begin to wake up throughout the ward.

"Team Ermine is eliminated, Top," she said into her device. "Their C2 is at the North entrance."

"Good work, Sergeant! *Angels' Wings* is now providing emergency backup power. This should allow the systems and critical devices to restart. But the medicoids will need to wait for full power to be functional.

"Have the Angels check their devices," he continued. "I have given you access to combat nursing modules that should allow you to support the medical staff until the hospital is fully operational."

"Yes, Top!" Zaza said. "Over and out!" Then she called the other Angels, "Angels, report!"

"Team Fisher is finished, Sarge!" said Sisi.

"Team Stoat has been stopped, Sarge!" said Tutu.

"Stand by, Troops!" Zaza said. Then she activated the combat nursing module on her device. She looked around quickly and took stock of the situation.

"Operation complete!" she said. "Check your devices, Ladies, and install the combat nursing modules, stat!"

•　　　•　　　•

After securing *Angels' Wings*, David loped toward the North entrance of the hospital. As he approached the last corner, he hugged the wall and peered around. He could see an armed terrorist keeping guard at the entrance. David raised the Corona-14, stepped around the corner, and fired. The man went up in flames and his body burst open from the extreme heat.

David sprinted toward the entrance. Another terrorist came around from the other side and raised a railgun to shoot, but David shot from the hip and the second man went down as well, engulfed in flames.

In the lobby, he saw the hospital staff prone on the floor with terrorists standing over them. As they started to raise their weapons, he depressed the trigger of the plasma rifle and swung it in a broad arc across the lobby, cutting down the terrorists, blazing a swath of incinerated flesh across their bodies. A man ducked down behind the counter. David walked around the counter and found the man curled up in a corner.

"The Hodfather tells us to strike down these crimes against nature!" the man railed, holding his hands palms out. "Hod will punish you for what you've done!"

"Let me enlighten you," David said, and blasted him with the Corona-14. The man burst into flames, for a brief moment screaming and thrashing. After he stopped moving, a cloud of greasy smoke streamed up, leaving a sooty stain on the ceiling.

•   •   •

The Angels consulted their devices and saw the new modules. As one, they triggered them.

"You rang?" said the Angels.

"Get scrubbed up, Ladies, and render assistance as needed!" Zaza said, with steel in her voice.

"Yes, Head Nurse!" the Angels said.

Zaza, Rara, and Bebe returned to the stock closet, found scrubs, and got changed. As they came out, Zaza looked at the deceased terrorists and said, "Better call for some body bags." Then they headed to the nursing station.

A handful of harried doctors were trying to consult the online records as the operations center came back online.

"Need some assistance?" Zaza said. "Just until the medicoids come back up?"

They looked at the Angels, looked at one another, and then said, "Head to the Intensive Care Unit. That's where they need the most help."

Zaza messaged the other Angels and they converged on the ICU. When they arrived, they found pandemonium as nurses and doctors were running from room to room trying to reconfigure and restart the medical devices that had gotten scrambled by the system going down.

"Looks serious," Zaza said. "Need some assistance?"

"Thank you!" one harried nurse said. "Find a nurse and lend a hand!"

The Angels each found a nurse to assist and jumped into the care. Sometimes it was just taking vitals or fetching equipment. Sometimes just holding the hand of terrified patients while the nurses and doctors tried to get life support devices working.

Zaza found herself holding the hand of a little girl who was in pain.

"It hurts! It hurts!" she sobbed.

"Look into my eyes," Zaza said, catching her gaze. Zaza smiled at her calmly. "You're going to be okay. They just have to get the machine reset and you're going to be alright. I promise! Hold on! Tight as you can!"

The little girl squeezed Zaza's hand and, a minute later, the machine began to administer the transdermal anesthetic. The nurse let out a deep breath and the little girl relaxed. Zaza brushed her sweaty hair back from her brow and followed the nurse to the next patient.

Bebe was paired with a nurse who was trying to perform phlebotomy, but was out of practice.

"Blast it!" she cursed as she missed the vein again. "Normally the medicoids do this!"

"May Bebe try?" Bebe said. The nurse looked doubtful, but stepped back. Bebe expertly applied the tourniquet, tapped the patient on the arm, and identified a vein.

"Bebe will give the patient just a little pinch," she said to the child who was gritting their teeth. But, in a moment, the needle was in and the vial was filled with blood.

"Bebe is all done!" she said, applying the bandage. "The patient was very brave!"

For more than an hour the Angels worked hard to support the efforts and, when full power finally came back on and the automated help began to function the nursing staff gave the Angels a cheer.

• • •

The Angels met David and Sssindy back in the Gender Affirming Clinic just before bed time. After hugging and sharing their stories with each other, they asked the staff if they could say good night to the children.

Sssindy and the Angels fanned out, still wearing their scrubs, and visited each child in their beds.

"Nighty-night, Patient!" they said. "Sweet dreams!"

The children smiled and yawned and let the Angels tuck them in.

Finally, they took the service elevator down to the loading dock and walked around the corner to where *Angels' Wings* was still at rest beside the backup generators. David disconnected the, now superfluous, auxiliary power cable and then went to trigger the cargo hatch, but as he did he tripped over the cable and fell, banging his knee.

Sssindy gasped.

David looked up at the Angels surrounding him, their eyes gleaming in the darkness.

"Please state the nature of your medical emergency, Patient," Zaza said.

"It's nothing," David said. "I just tripped."

"Is it critical?" asked Popo.

"Ooh, sounds serious," Rara said.

"Where does it hurt?" Sisi asked.

"Must be an emergency," Tutu said.

"It's really nothing," David insisted. "It's fine!"

"Bebe will take care of it," Bebe said.

The Angels grabbed him one on each arm, one on each leg, with the rest underneath him — and Bebe supporting his head. Then they carried him into *Angels' Wings* and took him to his bed. Sssindy followed anxiously, her tail vibrating with tension.

"Just relax and be compliant, Patient," Zaza said with a smile, snapping on some rubber gloves. "Nighty-night!"

THE BETTER ANGELS
AND
BEBE'S FIRST KISS

"**W**HO GOT YOUR FIRST KISS?" Sisi suddenly asked Sssindy. The Better Angels and Sssindy were all in the lounge of *Angels' Wings*, their starship that was currently docked in their permanent berth at the Truck Stop at the Center of the Galaxy.

Sssindy's tail started to vibrate. Sisi supposed Sssindy would be blushing, but since she was a giant, thicc, fluorescent pink snake, it was hard to tell just by looking at her. Her tail always gave her away, though.

"Why do you asssk, Sssweety?" she replied, nervously.

"Tell us! Tell us!" cried the rest of the Better Angels, who were always eager for love talk.

"Well, it's almost Valentine's Day," Sisi said. "So I just wondered."

"Well, then, tell me who got your firssst kissss," Sssindy said.

"Oh! Cap'n Tau got my first kiss," Sisi said, blushing.

"Captain Tau? Isss he in the military?" Sssindy asked.

"He's a starship pilot!" Sisi said. "David says he's the best pilot he's ever seen!"

"A ssstarsssship pilot!" Sssindy said. "He sssoundsss very dasssshing."

"Cap'n Tau took my first kiss too," Tutu said. "He knocked me down!"

"He knocked you down?" Sssindy asked, disturbed. "He sssoundsss violent!"

"He *stole* my first kiss," said Zaza, blushing.

"He ssstole your kissssss? Without consssent?"

"Me too," said all the other Angels in turn. "He stole my kiss too!"

"Really?" Sssindy asked, seriously perturbed. "Thisss Captain Tau isss bad newsss. He sssoundsss dangerousss."

"But, Bebe still hasn't had her first kiss, though," Bebe said.

"Well, you had better ssstay away from thisss Captain Tau!" Sssindy said.

The hatch buzzed and Bebe ran out to the door, shrieking, "Bebe will get it!"

She triggered the hatch and a giant tawny NeoBoxer with a black face sprang through the entrance and licked Bebe's face before she could react.

"Cap'n Tau!" she squealed. "You stole my first kiss!"

He spun in circles around her and then, as the other Angels came running over, he leapt among them licking their faces as well. Then he looked up at Sssindy, who drew herself up and stared down disapprovingly.

"You're not going to ssssteal my firssst kissssss," she hissed, then realized what she'd said.

The Angels all gasped. Bebe covered her mouth with her hands.

"You still haven't had your first kiss?" Zaza asked.

Sssindy looked embarrassed.

"I jusssst haven't met the right one yet," she said.

Captain Tau sat and waited while all of the Angels stood in a circle and watched. Sssindy's tail began to vibrate.

"Oh, alright ..." she said, finally, and Captain Tau jumped up and licked her face too.

THE BETTER ANGELS
AND
THE MILITARY MORALE MISHEGOSS

"**T**HIS IS PALISADE COMMAND," the speaker crackled. "We see you, *Angels' Wings*. You're cleared for landing."

Captain Tau barked and Sssindy, running comms, replied, "Five by five, Palisssade. *Angelsss' Wingsss* coming in hot."

The Better Angels had accepted a contract to visit military bases on the contested world of Palisade to raise morale of the troops. Humans had settled this planet only a hundred years ago, but an aggressive alien race that was trying to expand throughout the spiral arm had attacked, leaving the cities mostly in ruins. Although fighting was currently minimal, David had deemed it wise to engage Captain Tau to pilot *Angels' Wings*.

Captain Tau made a high-speed, powered descent toward the spaceport that had been converted into a giant military base.

David and the Angels were in Hold One where he was already in soldier mode, wearing a full set of body armor and carrying a long-range *Ublyudok* particle rifle and scope. The Angels milled around cheerfully, wearing their pink-and-blue magical-girl costumes, waiting for the all clear so they could open the cargo hatch and meet their fans.

"*Angelsss' Wingsss* isss down," Sssindy announced.

David shouldered the *Ublyudok* and climbed the ladder up to the top hatch. Before the ship was a sea of military personnel standing in ranks, waiting for the Angels. David scanned the full horizon and then took up a position overlooking the cargo hatch.

"All clear," he announced.

The cargo hatch opened, and the Better Angels emerged to deafening cheers from the soldiers. With Sssindy running comms, Zaza took the lead and, waving her arms, yelled, "Are you ready, Palisade?"

The crowd screamed with approval and the Better Angels moved seamlessly into their routine, singing and dancing. They performed a selected set of famous PuzzyCure songs, beginning with *Pilots' Blues*, then the hysterically funny *Soldiers' Lament*, followed by the sing-along *Navy Life*:

Oh, the Cap'n of the starship,
he's got a nasty bark!
And when he bites your ketsu,
it leaves a nasty mark!

Oh-no-no I'm so done with all this navy life!
Hey, Top, just let me jump home!

The soldiers were screaming with laughter, and they were about to sing the next stanza when sirens sounded across the base.

"'pedes incoming!" was blasted over the loudspeakers.

The soldiers, with good discipline, began to scatter to their positions. The Angels fell back to the cargo hatch. Captain Tau started the engines which first whined and then grew to a grumbling roar. David from his perch, spotted movement coming from the west.

"'pedes on the base!" he reported, and took aim with his *Ublyudok*.

The 'pede soldier morph was a large centipede-like creature. They had little intelligence and carried no weapons, but were vicious and single-minded. They were highly flattened with thick exoskeletons, huge pincers, and many legs, that could roll at great speed like a hoop. There were dozens rolling across the tarmac toward *Angels' Wings*.

David fired the *Ublyudok,* which emitted a deafening scream, and hit five 'pedes in rapid succession. But there were many more coming. Missile volleys began to streak into the sky from all around the spaceport as fighter spacecraft appeared and began to rake the field with beam weapons. The spacecraft were flown by the soft, grub-like 'pede officer morph. They were highly intelligent, devilishly clever, and cunning pilots, but were never seen in ground assaults and had only been described when their corpses were recovered from crashed spacecraft.

The Angels were aboard and David threw himself into the hatch on the roof, dogged it, and then slid down the ladder.

"Go! Go! Go!" he called.

"Ssstrap yoursssselvesss in, Angelsss!" Sssindy called.

Captain Tau barked and pushed the throttle to full. *Angels' Wings* lifted off and accelerated fast, headed east at low altitude.

Two fighters peeled off and began to pursue *Angels' Wings*. Captain Tau flew nap-of-the-land, just above the treetops, taking evasive action whenever sensors detected weapons locking on. But he was unable to shake the pursuers. Growling, he headed toward the ruins of the largest city.

He flew up a wide river just above the surface of the water, zigging and zagging erratically. The pursuers stuck tight. A huge rail suspension bridge loomed overhead. Tau suddenly swerved and flew under the bridge at an acute angle, cutting sharply between two support pillars. One pursuer slammed into a support and exploded in a spectacular burst of flames. The other tried to overfly the bridge, but clipped the top, spinning out of control. Before aerodynamic forces tore it apart, its beam weapon engaged and raked *Angels' Wings*, striking an engine and the fuselage.

Klaxons started to scream on the bridge.

"Damage report," Sssindy said, her tail vibrating but keeping her voice calm. "Port engine flameout and hull compromisssed."

Streaming smoke, *Angels' Wings* streaked over the blasted city. Captain Tau fought the controls and turned toward an abandoned refinery, where he set down among the cracking and fractionating columns, piping, and old flare stack, all now idle. Tau sat panting and then whined as the engines wound down.

David came onto the bridge.

"That was some masterful flying, Cap'n," he said. "You're the best pilot I've ever seen and that's really saying something."

Tau's tongue lolled at the compliment.

"Angels," David announced. "It's time to get jacked up!

"Tutu! Lala! Nene! You're the repair team. I've just made the combat engineer modules available to you. Identify the damaged components, replicate, and install them!"

"On it, Top!"

"Sisi! You lead reconnaissance! Grab the other *Ublyudok*, get railguns for Mumu, Popo, and Rara and take up a position at the top of the flare stack to be ready to hold off any 'pedes!

"Yes, Top!" Sisi said.

"Are you gonna give Bebe orders?" Bebe asked.

"You and Zaza grab the Corona-14s and stay close to guard the repair team."

"They'll have to go through Bebe, Top!"

"Where will you be, Master Sergeant?" Zaza asked.

"I'll be up top again."

"Understood!" Zaza barked. "Let's move, Bebe!"

In only moments, the Angels were armed and deployed. David took up his position on the top of *Angels' Wings* and motioned for the reconnaissance team to move. They headed across the rubble-strewn ground and scaled the flare stack.

Zaza and Bebe stood close in with the Corona-14s while Tutu and Nene removed the cowling and began to disassemble the engine to identify and remove the damaged components.

"Gimme a MQ32 torsion wrench," Tutu said, her head buried in the engine, holding out her hand. Nene slapped it into her palm.

Lala ran the replicator and began to bring replacement parts out.

"Here's the QR45 port manifold ducting element!" she said.

"We need the RS2185 manifold coupling first!"

"On it!" Lala said, running back to the replicator.

"'pedes at 10 o'clock!" Sisi announced, and began to fire her *Ublyudok*. The rifle made a series of screaming reports that echoed among the columns and superstructure of the ruined refinery.

David tried to see where they were coming from, but wasn't high enough at first. Then he saw them come slithering over the rubble.

"At least they can't roll here," he said, as he opened fire himself.

There were still ten that got within sight of Zaza and Bebe who opened fire with their plasma rifles. The 'pedes burst into flames, spraying bits of burning exoskeleton and writhing as they died.

Lala's voice came over the communicator. "The replicator is running short on iron. Can you grab some scrap iron and feed it into the recycler?"

"Bebe is on it!" Bebe and Zaza slung their Corona-14s and collected scrap pieces of sheet metal and chunks of rebar lying among the rubble strewn across the landscape. They hustled them into the recycler. Just as they reached the recycler, they heard Tutu and Nene scream.

"'pedes are coming up from under Angels' Wings! They're coming up through tunnels!"

Zaza and Bebe ran back outside and roasted a couple of 'pedes that showed themselves, but they could see that there were more down in the tunnels.

"It would be suicide to go down in there, Top," Zaza said. "But if we don't do something fast, they'll be able to attack us at will."

Something pink dove through the cargo hatch and then flashed past Zaza and Bebe. They ran over and looked down just in time to see Sssindy slither down and vanish into a tunnel.

"Good hunting, Sssindy!" Zaza called after her.

"Bebe says to watch your tail!" Bebe whispered.

Sssindy erected her fangs and bit the first 'pede she encountered, injecting only a small amount of venom, conserving as much as possible. The 'pede tried to get a hold of her with its pincers but, losing strength, they slid off her scales. She slithered forward into the tunnel until she found a junction and coiled up, blocking the way forward. The 'pedes farther back, charged at her. She hissed and made abortive strikes to keep them pushed back, biting only when necessary. Their writhing corpses piled up in front of her as she bought precious minutes for the repair team.

Lala, running back and forth, ferried out the rest of the newly replicated components. Tutu and Nene replaced the damaged parts as fast as they could and reassembled the engine. They skipped replacing the cowling, and switched to replacing the damaged hull plates. Tightening the last bolts, Tutu called, "We are spaceworthy and go for liftoff."

"'pedes are coming!" Sisi cried and repeated screaming reports of her *Ublyudok* echoed across the site.

David whistled when he saw that a veritable wave of 'pedes was pouring across the rubble from all directions. He too began to shoot as fast as he could line up targets.

"Fire up the engines, Cap'n!" he shouted. "Right now!"

Captain Tau barked and started the engines. Sisi and the recon team watched with horror as the wave passed them and dozens of 'pedes began scaling the flare stack. Mumu, Popo, and Rara shot down with their rail guns, trying to keep the swarm from reaching the top and overwhelming them.

As the horde approached *Angels' Wings*, 'pedes began boiling up out of more openings from the tunnels.

Zaza and Bebe stood their ground with the Corona-14s, roasting 'pedes and providing covering fire until Sssindy, emerged like pink lightning up out of the tunnels and threw herself into the cargo hatch, just as *Angels' Wings* started to lift off.

Dozens of 'pedes were scaling the sides of *Angels' Wings* as Captain Tau carefully swung the hovering spacecraft toward the flare stack. Zaza slung her Corona-14, climbed up the ladder to the top hatch, and stood back-to-back with David who was picking off any 'pedes that made it to the top. But then a wave swarmed toward him *en masse*, she swung the Corona-14 in a broad arc, roasting them.

Panting with tension, Captain Tau maneuvered *Angels' Wings* delicately, orienting the cargo hatch toward the flare stack. Bebe blasted the climbing 'pedes with her plasma rifle to keep them from reaching the top while the recon team climbed onto the railing, 30 meters above the ground, and leapt through the air into the cargo hatch. Bebe slapped the hatch control.

"Angels aboard!" she cried. "Bebe has sealed the hatch!"

"Get inside, Top!" Zaza cried, as she roasted another rush of 'pedes.

"Yes, ma'am!" he said, slinging the *Ublyudok* and dropping through the hatch.

Zaza fired one more blast then jumped inside herself while David pulled the hatch down and dogged it closed again as the 'pedes swarmed just above.

"Get us out of here, Cap'n!" he cried.

Captain Tau opened the throttle wide and, with a roar, *Angels' Wings* cast herself skyward. As she picked up speed, the 'pedes clinging to the hull were peeled off and fell back, while they swarmed and seethed across the whole site. Captain Tau barked as they cleared the atmosphere. Sssindy streaked into the bridge, taking up the comm console again.

"Palisssade Control, *Angelsss' Wingsss* isss go for jump,"

"We read you *Angels' Wings*. Thanks for the show. We'll have you back for the rest of the tour once things settle down."

"Roger that. *Angelsss' Wingsss* out."

David and the Angels were all lying on the mats in Hold One, still shaking and panting with the exertion, when *Angels' Wings* went to jump.

David and Zaza rolled over and regarded one another.

"Let's not stand down just yet, Sergeant," David said. "Just in case."

"Affirmative, Top. No hurry."

THE BETTER ANGELS
AND
THE COMPLICATED CAMPING
CATASTROPHE

DAVID RETURNED TO *Angels' Wings* on the Truck Stop at the Center of the Galaxy to find the spaceway on the Docking Ring surrounded by the small Truck Stop emergency vehicles with flashing lights. He could see Sssindy and the Better Angels standing (or lying) outside looking sad, among a crowd of firefighters and emergency personnel. He broke into a run.

"What's happened?" he asked, when he arrived.

"There was a fire onboard the starship," the Fire Chief said. "The fire suppression system engaged automatically and we were called to respond."

"How did the fire start?" David asked.

"I'll let them answer that," the Chief said, nodding at the Angels.

David turned to the Angels. They looked miserably at the deck and wouldn't meet his eyes.

"Well?" he asked.

"It was my fault, David," Zaza said, sorrowfully.

"No! It was Bebe's fault!" Bebe shouted.

"It was my fault! It was my fault!" the rest all said.

"Tell me what happened!"

"We were watching a show about camping girls," Zaza explained.

"And they made s'mores!" Bebe said.

"So we tried to make some," Zaza concluded.

"So ..." David said, grasping for the thread here. "So you tried to make a campfire?"

"Just a little one!"

David rolled his eyes, sighed, and then entered *Angels' Wings* to get a sense of the damage. There was fire suppression foam everywhere. He waded through it to get into the lounge and there he found the remains of a small campfire in the middle of the room. He sighed again and went back out.

"I'm really sorry, David," Zaza said.

"Bebe is very, very sorry," Bebe said.

"Well, there's only one thing for it," he said. "Until *Angels' Wings* is cleaned, restored, and livable again, you Angels are going to have to go camping."

The Angels looked up and David watched as their expressions transformed from sadness and sheepishness to wonderment and then excitement.

"Will Bebe get to make s'mores?"

"Yes," David said. "We will be certain to find a camp where Bebe will get to make s'mores."

The Angels all cheered.

"Where are *you* going to go?" Sssindy asked David, her tail vibrating with tension. "And where can I go? Where can I ssstay on the Truck Ssstop?"

"I think I'll go to the Select Club. But that won't work for you since you're not ex-military. Let's check with the Zoological Sanctuary. They should be able to find a place for you for a few days."

"Ooh!" Sssindy said breathlessly. "Thisss isss ssstarting to sssound like a vacation!"

•   •   •

David led the Angels to the branch office of the *Gyarakushīsukautos* in the Blue Sector of the Truck Stop. The walls of the lobby were huge displays showing girls engaged in all kinds of outdoor activities.

The Angels were captivated and stopped in their tracks, staring around with wonder and excitement. David stepped forward to the counter. Behind the counter, a matronly woman wearing a tan uniform and cap looked up.

"May I help you?"

"We would like to send them to summer camp."

"The Better Angels want to go camping?" she marveled.

"Yes," David said. "And we need a camp where they'll be able to make s'mores." Bebe, who'd been engrossed, watching the displays, suddenly perked up as though she'd heard her name.

"There's a camp just starting on Daphnae-3," the woman said. "I think there's still room." She looked kindly at Bebe. "And don't worry, little one. We always get to make s'mores."

Bebe beamed and the Angels all cheered.

"Now, before I sign you up for your camping adventure, let's settle a few details," the woman said. "Are you sure you want to go as the Better Angels?

"Is there anything wrong with that?" Zaza asked.

"Well, idols sometimes find that people treat you differently if they know you're famous. But if you wear scouting uniforms and use assumed names, you can have the same experience as all the other girls."

David and Zaza exchanged glances. David could see that the idea appealed to her.

"What will you call yourselves?" David asked.

"How about we say we're ... What do you call it when there are nine twins?"

"Nonuplets," David said.

"And our names can be Banya, Lanya, Manya, Nanya, Panya, Ranya, Sanya, Tanya, and Zanya!"

"Bebe loves this idea!" Bebe said, pumping her fist.

David and Zaza looked at one another and shook their heads. Zaza took Bebe aside.

"Bebe, we're going to go *incognito*," she said.

"Bebe understands!" Bebe said, pumping her fist again.

"That means you can't tell anyone your real name."

"Bebe has got it!" Bebe said triumphantly.

Zaza sighed and let it go.

"Before you go," the older woman said, "Let's get you outfitted with scouting uniforms and everything else you'll need for camping. There's a liner leaving for Daphnae-3 in two hours! That's just enough time to get everything squared away."

David watched while she quickly entered line after line of data into the billing system.

"Now, I'll just need your thumb impression here ..."

David looked down the row of figures and then at the total and tried to count the number of digits. Finally, he gave up and just pressed his thumb and the device made a soft chime when he accepted the charges.

"Now, come along, Gyarus!" she called, directing them into the back of the office. "There's not a moment to lose!"

"Good luck, Angels!" David called after them.

"Ssh! Ssh!" they shushed him, grinning. "We're Gyarus now!"

But then they all hugged him and he stayed long enough to watch them get taken back to be outfitted for their adventure. Then David departed walking briskly antispinward.

•   •   •

David entered the Select Club in the Red Zone of the Truck Stop. It had a quiet, understated atmosphere, with soft carpet and dark paneling. The Chamberlain, behind the counter, recognized him immediately and nodded to him.

"Welcome back, David," he said. "We haven't seen you for a while."

"I'll need to stay for a few days," David said. He tapped his device on the counter and received the access credential for sleeping quarters. Then he entered the lounge. It was half full with the ex-military types that the club catered to.

There were a half-dozen tables with small groups of ex-soldiers. As was typical, the tables were segregated by rank: some had officers, having quiet conversation and drinking brandy or wine, while others were enlisted men, engaged in raucous banter over glasses of beer and whiskey. David found an unoccupied table off to the side and went to sit down.

"Who's that guy?" someone said, loudly, pointing. He was sitting at one of the loudest tables with a band of rough-looking enlisted men. "He doesn't belong here."

"Hey you!" the man said, standing and pointing at David directly. "What unit did you serve in?"

David just looked at the man and then took his seat at the table.

"Hey! I'm talking to you!" the man said, approaching David's table. He was a large man, with a livid burn scar on his face. David looked up at him, unruffled. The Chamberlain hurried over.

"Excuse me, Gunny," he said. "The Master Sergeant has every right to be here."

"Him?" the Gunnery Sergeant snorted. "A Master Sergeant? I don't believe it! I challenge that!"

David stood. "Marksmanship," he said, quietly. "With the *Mottusuchi*."

"I'll judge," said an elderly man at an officer's table, coming to his feet.

"Thanks, General," the Chamberlain said. He collected a suitcase from behind the counter and then led the three men back to the firing range. From the suitcase, he extracted a *Mottusuchi* pin beam — a brutal looking firearm constructed of stamped metal parts with little artistry or attention to aesthetics: a pure and single-minded killing machine.

The Gunnery Sergeant carefully sighted the pin beam at the target and fired. The weapon made no sound, but a tiny hole, the size of a pencil lead, was burned through the paper target in the bullseye, but slightly off center. The range registered the shot.

"Beat that!" he crowed.

David took the *Mottusuchi* and, casually depressing the trigger, fired from the hip. Then, without looking at the result, he handed it back to the Chamberlain and walked away.

"Wait!" the Gunnery Sergeant said, exasperated. "You didn't even hit the target!"

"Yes, he did, Gunny," the General said. "He fired through the hole you made."

The Gunnery Sergeant just stood there, floored, as he checked the system and determined that it was as the General said.

"Don't feel bad, son," the General said, clapping him on the shoulder. "Nobody has ever beaten the Master Sergeant at marksmanship."

•   •   •

Traveling incognito, the Better Angels arrived at the spaceport where they disembarked from the passenger liner and were collected together with several girls headed to the *Gyarakushīsukauto* summer camp. A cheerful young man with a bushy beard, wearing a *Gyarakushīsukauto* uniform, appeared and waved his arms.

"Gyarus! Come over here! My name is Koguma and I will be one of the Counselors during the camping week! Let me check my list to make sure I've got everyone."

He got out his device and began to call out names.

"Banya!"

"Bebe is here!" Bebe said.

Zaza covered her face and shook her head but Koguma just scratched his head and continued with "Ĉiaki!"

"Here," a short, pudgy girl said.

"Lanya!"

"Here!"

"Lin!"

"Here!" said a taller, dark-haired girl.

"Manya!

"Here!"

"Nadeŝko!"

"That's me!" said a curvy red-headed girl.

He went through the rest of the list. Then he looked around at the Angels.

"Are you all sisters or something?"

"Yes, we're nonuplets," Zaza said.

"Wow! That's so cool!" Koguma said. "Now that we've got everyone, let's head to the transport to take you to Camp *Gyarakushīsukauto*!"

He led his charges to another gate of the spaceport where they went down stairs onto the tarmac where a yellow Makasete SkyJumper was parked.

As they lined up to board the SkyJumper, Nadeŝko turned to Zaza.

"You look familiar for some reason," she said. "Have we met before? Maybe at camp last year?"

"I don't think so," Zaza said. "We've never been camping before."

"Oh! You're in for a treat!" she gushed. "The *Gyarakushīsukautos* are the best! This is my third year coming, but I'll be too old next year. How old are you?"

"We're twelve," Zaza said, repeating the false information they'd constructed for their cover identities. She couldn't very well tell Nadeŝko that they'd been molecularly assembled less than a year ago.

The Gyarus entered the SkyJumper and sat on bench seats, two on each side of the aisle. Koguma sat in the pilot seat and pressed the button. The SkyJumper lifted off and flew at low altitude for 20 minutes toward snow-capped mountains before descending into a forested valley near a large lake.

•　　　•　　　•

The camp was situated in a picturesque setting. A cluster of rustic wooden buildings was located along the shore of a deep, clear lake set within a vast forest. They stepped off the transport, looking around in wonder, and joined a huge crowd of Gyarus already there who were milling about in an open grassy field.

"Bebe wants to go swimming!" Bebe said.

"Ssh! Ssh!" the other Angels hushed. "Don't say your name!"

"Bebe can't help it!" she pouted.

Once everyone had arrived, an older woman wearing a scouting uniform climbed up on a platform with a headset.

"Can everyone hear me? Welcome to Camp *Gyarakushīsukauto*! Are you ready to blast off?"

There were excited cheers from the assembled girls and the Angels joined in enthusiastically.

"We have a full week of exciting activities — swimming, canoeing, archery, hiking, orienteering, as well as the feminine arts — and by the end of the week you'll all be experienced, seasoned Gyarus!"

"But finally," the Camp Leader announced. "All campers must surrender their devices for the duration of the camp. You're here to experience the natural environment, the physical activities, and the comradeship of one another, so no distractions from outside the camp are allowed. Thank you! And have a wonderful week!"

After the announcements, the Angels lined up with the other Gyarus to surrender their devices to Koguma. Zaza made a quick adjustment on hers before she handed it over.

"Here is my device, as requisitioned, Civ... I mean, Counselor," she said. Koguma accepted it, affixed a label, then glanced up and was transfixed by Zaza's direct and murderous gaze. He shivered for a moment.

"Thank you ..." he said, glancing at her name tag. "Zanya." He wrote her name on the label and deposited the device in the box with the others.

•   •   •

A small crowd of people in the Green Sector was waiting for the elevator as it arrived at the Main Ring from the Docking Ring. There was a quiet chime and the doors slid open, then there were shrieks and cries of dismay as a 10-meter long, thicc, fluorescent pink snake uncoiled herself from the cramped elevator and slithered out.

"Excussse me! Pardon me! Pleassse let me through! Excussse me!" Sssindy said, as people recoiled trying to get out of the way. Sssindy slithered spinward, attracting stares until she reached the Zoological Sanctuary.

"Sssindy!" Lusa called, as she slithered in the door. "What brings you here?"

"*Angelsss' Wingsss* is being repaired and I'm looking for a place to ssstay for a few days," she said, anxiously, her tail beating a tattoo on the deck. "David sssuggesssted that maybe I could ssstay here."

"Sure!" Lusa said. "It will be fine for you to stay in the Zoological Sanctuary for a few days — if you don't mind just sleeping on the grass."

"Oh, thank goodnesssss!" Sssindy said, with relief. "Itsss hard to find sssuitable quartersss in the Truck Ssstop."

Lusa held the door and invited Sssindy out into the Zoological Sanctuary. They headed across the open grassy field and Lusa gestured to a stand of bamboo. "If you go behind here, you can probably have a little privacy. Though watch out, because sometimes Tau goes back there."

There was a scurry of yellow in the vegetation. Lusa cursed and shook her fist.

"Those blasted magarats are everywhere!"

She saw another when a blur of pink lashed out and snagged the magarat. Sssindy picked it up, squealing & struggling, and tossed it back like a piece of candy. A bulge moved down her throat to her stomach.

"It'sss a little bitter," Sssindy said. "But it'sss not a bad sssnack."

"Ooh!" Lusa said, rubbing her hands. "Can you catch more? The Zoological Sanctuary will pay you for every one you eat!"

•   •   •

The Angels spent the afternoon getting settled into their tents. They were organized four to a tent with three Angels and another girl in each tent: Lala, Mumu, and Tutu had Ĉiaki; Popo, Rara, and Sisi had Lin; and Bebe, Nene, and Zaza had Nadeŝko. Once they were settled in, it was time for dinner. And after dinner, they sat around the campfire to tell stories. The Angels listened attentively while the other girls told stories about other camping trips they'd taken. When it was her turn, Sisi started to describe their recent terrifying adventure on Palisade.

"And there we were! Surrounded by 'pedes!" Sisi said. The girls all drew in their breath.

"You're a liar!" Ĉiaki shouted. "You've never seen a real, live 'pede! I have!"

"Sis ... Sanya is telling the truth!" Bebe said. "Bebe was there too!"

"Affirmative. We were all there, Civ... Ĉiaki," Zaza stated. "We barely escaped."

The other Angels murmured and nodded assent.

"I'm sorry," Ĉiaki said into the awkward silence. "I lived on Palisade ... Before the 'pedes came."

She covered her face with her hands and sobbed to remember.

"There, there," Bebe said, patting her back. "Bebe is sorry too.

At that moment, Koguma walked up, carrying armfuls of supplies.

"Who wants to make s'mores?" Koguma said.

"Bebe does! Bebe does!" Bebe shrieked. All of the other Gyarus clamored as well.

•   •   •

David walked to the HandyCare Detailing and Restoration Service office in the Blue Sector. An older man with white hair and a mustache, wearing soiled, rumpled clothes stood behind the counter. He was looking at a screen on the counter and didn't seem to notice when David entered.

David cleared his throat. The man continued looking at his screen, evincing no evidence that he was aware of David's presence. David sighed. He hated dealing with people.

"Excuse me," David said finally.

"Hah?" the man said, finally looking up.

"Excuse me," David repeated. "I'm here to see what the repair and cleaning charge is for *Angels' Wings*."

"What?" the man said.

"*Angels' Wings*. The spacecraft. You're supposed to have an estimate of the cost for me."

"Oooh! Gotcha!" the man said. He looked at his screen and began mumbling to himself. "No. Right. That. And that. Fourteen. Carry the six. There!"

He indicated a screen that showed a long list of charges. David scrolled down and down and down and winced when he finally saw the total.

"It seems expensive," David murmured.

"Hah?" the man said.

"It seems expensive," David stated again, louder.

"Well, those old DR-420s have one of them AS41 fire suppression systems. They really do the job, but ya almost can't find that agent to recharge 'em with no more — it's military, ya know! But I know a guy who knows a guy and we can get ya some. I'll tell ya this, though — you'd be a whole lot unhappier if you had to replace that whole fire suppression system with a new one."

David sighed again and then took a deep breath and pressed his thumb against the screen, which chimed accepting the charge.

"Welp, it's been a pleasure doin' bidness with ya!" the guy said. "We'll get right on it just as soon as we can. Shouldn't take more'n a few days!"

•   •   •

After Lusa departed, Sssindy took a deep breath, coiled up, and relaxed in the Zoological Sanctuary behind the bamboo. Visitors wandered through every so often, so she laid still and let people ooh and aah and point. Eventually visiting hours ended and they started to turn down the lighting, simulating sunset and nightfall.

As the artificial sunlight was decreased, Sssindy decided to go hunting. She slithered through the grass, testing the scent with her tongue. She could smell the trails where the magarats had run before. She followed a trail toward a back corner of the sanctuary. As she approached, another magarat popped out through a loose panel in the wall. She grabbed it. It squeaked as she tossed it back and swallowed it. She settled down for a bit and after a few minutes another came out and yet another. But then they stopped.

She waited for a while. She could smell more behind the loose panel. A magarat pushed the panel out with its snout and Sssindy flashed forward, catching it and getting her head inside the panel. After she swallowed that one, she gradually forced her way inside the panel. She barely fit through the opening, but she managed it and found herself inside a warren of interstitial spaces behind the walls of the space station. It was very dark, but Sssindy was used to dark spaces, having spent months hiding in interior spaces of the Ironball to avoid *La Menageriste*. She tested the air with her tongue, waving the forks this way and that, then she began to slither toward where the odor of the magarats was strongest.

As she moved forward, she sensed a gathering of them up ahead. And something larger. They suddenly charged her, trying to bite. She erected her fangs and began to bite as many as quickly as possible, injecting only a small amount of venom. The bitten rats, staggered off, and dropped, but there were dozens. She got many small bites, but eventually, all of the worker magarats were bitten and dead or dying. But farther back was the queen of the magarat nest. She was huge and formidable.

They circled, feinting at one another in the dark. She would charge and then draw back, leaving Sssindy striking at empty air. After one such strike, she sprang forward again and nearly got her teeth into Sssindy's neck just behind her head. Sssindy's tail vibrated with frustration. Then Sssindy realized that in circling, she had gotten between the queen and her brood. She feinted a strike at the mewling kits and when the queen, enraged, charged blindly in, Sssindy turned in a flash and struck her, injecting a massive dose of venom. And then she threw a loop of her body around the queen and began to constrict.

Weakened by the venom, the queen finally succumbed. It took a long time, but Sssindy swallowed her too. Then she ate the brood of kits and all of the worker magarats she had killed before, carefully keeping count so she could demand fair compensation. Finally, fully sated, she settled down in the empty nest for a quiet night's sleep.

•   •   •

After breakfast, the Angels' troop of Gyarus was signed up to do orienteering. The SkyJumper, with the windows made opaque, carried the Gyarus to a remote location and dropped them off with plenty of water and a map and a compass. And Koguma got off with them to observe.

"Don't expect me to tell you Gyarus where we are, though," he said. "You have to figure that out yourselves!"

They spread the map out on the ground and crowded around it.

"Let me try," said Nadeŝko. She laid the compass on the map, studied the map, and then looked around. The Gyarus all watched her attentively.

"There are mountain peaks here and here," she said, indicating the map. Then she pointed, "Those must be those mountains there and there.

"So we must be about here," she concluded, indicating a location on the map. "That means, we should go that way to get back to camp."

"Ooh! Bebe thinks you're really smart!" Bebe said.

Nadeŝko blushed at the compliment.

"Let's saddle up!" Zaza growled.

They started to hike toward the camp in the dappled shade of the forest. The birds were singing and it was a glorious day with a light breeze, and many wildflowers were in bloom. They chattered among themselves, pointing out interesting trees, plants, and rocks. But then they reached a spot where the way was blocked by a landslide. There was a broad swath of loose rock and scree that looked unstable — too dangerous to cross. They consulted the map.

"Why don't we go this way?" Lin said, indicating the map. "If we try to go around that way, we'll end up in this swamp. And there's steep relief over there. This way is a little longer, but it looks safer."

"Bebe thinks you're pretty smart too!" Bebe said. Lin beamed at the compliment and they set off downslope in a different direction. The forest became darker and denser. In places, they had to detour around thickets and dense vegetation. Without visual landmarks, they had to consult the compass more frequently to make sure they were staying on the heading they had selected. After an hour, they emerged into a clearing where they found a walled compound constructed out of ugly pre-fabricated metal sheeting surrounded by barbed-wire fencing with signs warning of electric shock. At the corners of the compound were guard towers.

"Nobody move!" a voice commanded.

A squad of armed men wearing body armor and carrying railguns emerged from all sides surrounding them.

"We're *Gyarakushīsukautos* from the camp on an orienteering exercise! We're just ..." Koguma started to say when one of the men shoved a railgun in his gut. He huffed with the wind knocked out of him.

"Bebe says to leave him alone!" Bebe shouted.

"Silence!" the man snarled. He shoved the railgun in Bebe's face.

"Now is not the time, Civ... Banya," Zaza said, raising her hands.

Bebe raised her hands too and slowly backed away.

"You'll only be detained until we confirm your identities," the leader said. He motioned with the railgun. "Hands over your head! March!"

The troop of Gyarus was marched through the gate and into the facility.

•　　•　　•

"Here is your 'Fun Meal,' Master Sergeant," the waiter said with disgust, depositing a small box on David's table.

There were quiet chuckles from all around, but when David looked up, everyone maintained solemn expressions — except for a woman wearing a leather jacket at the bar who winked. She walked over and joined him at the table.

"I should have known it would be you, Captain Reckless," he said.

"It's been a long time, Master Sergeant," she said with a throaty whisper.

He opened the box, unwrapped the sandwich, and took a bite.

"What? I thought you hated those!"

"You get used to them," David said.

She leaned forward over the table, practically inviting him to look down her shirt, and reached a hand out toward David's cheek. "I'm really glad to see you, you know."

David took another bite of his Fun Meal and met her gaze.

She leaned back and stretched her arms up over her head, in a languorous, lissome gesture that emphasized her charms.

"You know that has no effect on me," David said.

She pouted, then grinned.

"That's what I like about you, David. All business." She sat back and regarded him seriously. "I have a proposition for you."

"I don't do that kind of work anymore," David said.

"It's lucrative ..." she purred.

"You aren't listening to me, Racy," David reiterated. "I don't do that kind of work anymore."

He took another bite of his fun meal.

"But this is a milk run! A simple extraction of a political prisoner from an internment camp on Daphnae-3."

David choked.

"Daphnae-3?" he asked.

"Yep. Just a hop, skip, and a jump away."

David vacillated, weighing probabilities. What were the chances the Angels had gotten mixed up in something? They were only there for a week. And it was a whole planet! But, he considered further, playing devil's-advocate with himself, we're talking about the Angels here. He decided.

"I'm in," he said. "Let's go. I don't have access to my ship, so we'll need to take yours. And I'll need to equip myself before we go."

"No problem," Captain Reckless said. "Why don't you get what you need from the Select Club. They'll rent it to you at very reasonable rates!"

•　　　•　　　•

The Gyarus were separated from Koguma and each other, each placed alone in a tiny cell. Zaza paced around like a caged animal, flexing her hands into fists. Then she heard something. She pressed her ear to the door listening for any clues. Straining, far down the hall, she could just barely overhear the guards talking.

"Which one shall we start with?"

"Let's take that mouthy one. She seems like she'll be easy to break."

Zaza heard them approach and then unlock a door.

"Come along, you!" the guard ordered. "You're going to answer some questions."

"Bebe will tell you nothing!" Bebe spat.

"Move!" the guard ordered. Zaza heard the guard grab Bebe's uniform and drag her out.

Bebe let out a squeak and then footsteps receded down the passageway, punctuated now and again with another scuffle and another cry. Finally a door closed far down the hallway and there was silence.

Zaza's blood boiled with rage. She began to pant with agitation and suppressed fury. She had never been so angry. She closed her eyes and invested a few moments in deep breathing to calm herself down. Then she began to systematically search the tiny cell for weaknesses or some way to escape.

•　　　•　　　•

David went to the counter in the Select Club. The Chamberlain looked up.

"I need to rent some equipment," David said.

"We charge standard rates," the Chamberlain replied. "What are you looking for?"

David thought for a moment and then said, "I'll need a full set of body armor. And why don't I take that *Mottusuchi*. I haven't used one of those for a long time and I think it may be just what I need on this job."

The Chamberlain made a few entries and showed David the total. He whistled. But, after just a moment, he pressed his thumb to the sensor and accepted the charges.

"I sure hope this job pays as well as Racy says it does," he thought as he collected the two suitcases from the Chamberlain containing the body armor and pin beam. He returned to the lounge.

"Ready?" Racy said, downing the last swallow of her drink. "Let's boost!"

They headed toward the elevators down to the Docking Ring.

"I don't suppose you know someone who could run comms for us," she said.

"As it happens, I do. You're not afraid of snakes, are you?"

•   •   •

The guard pushed Bebe into the darkened interrogation chamber and then pressed her into a hard metal chair. A bright light snapped on, focused on her face. She blinked trying to see. In front of her was a small table.

A man behind the table, silhouetted against the light, consulted a device and then looked up.

"Your entry documentation states you are Banya Angeli. Is that correct?"

"Bebe will not answer your questions," Bebe said. "Bebe will tell you nothing."

"So you admit that you're not Banya Angeli?"

"Bebe admits nothing."

A man came into the room and whispered to the interrogator. He leaned forward over the table.

"Our scans say you're not even human. You're a biological android! Where's your programming interface, android?"

Bebe crossed her arms and maintained a steely silence.

"I demand you reveal your programming interface. Let's see just who you answer to."

The corners of Bebe's mouth turned up just a tiny bit.

"Compel the rogue android!" the interrogator said to the technician. He consulted his device.

"I can't. Her interface is locked down tight. You'd have to do a full wipe. We don't have the equipment for that and we'd lose all the data."

"Go get that other one. She seemed to listen to her. Maybe she can talk some sense into her. Or she might be open to a little coercion if her friend is threatened."

They were surprised when Bebe finally spoke up.

"Listen to Bebe," she said, in a singsong voice. "You're about to make a really big mistake. If you try to hurt anyone, Bebe won't be sorry when you're all dead."

"Go get her! Now!"

•   •   •

David and Racy arrived at the Zoological Sanctuary.

"Is Sssindy here?" David asked Lusa.

"Yes!" she said. "She came yesterday. I think she's back behind the bamboo."

They walked across the grassy meadow and looked behind the bamboo, but there was no thicc fluorescent pink serpent. They cast about for a while and then heard quiet cursing coming from the back corner. They pushed through the vegetation and found Sssindy's head and neck protruding through an opening in the wall.

"Good morning, Sssindy!" David said.

"Oh! Oh! Thank goodnessss you're here!" she said. "I'm ssstuck!"

David started to laugh, but Racy and Lusa shushed him fiercely. "It's not funny to laugh at a lady in such a circumstance!"

"How did you even get in there?" he asked.

"I followed the magaratsss back to their nessst," she said. "But then I ate them all and now I can't get out!"

"You ate them? All?" Lusa asked. "That's fantastic! How many were there."

"There were sssixty-three workersss plus fourteen kitsss. And the queen."

Lusa whistled. "That's a tidy sum. The Zoological Sanctuary will pay."

"Something's come up," David said. "Racy and I need you to run comms for us."

"Well, just help me get out of here!"

David opened a suitcase and pulled out the *Mottusuchi*.

"Don't move," he said. He made a quick semi-circular gesture with the pinbeam and cut a thin line through a section of the wall. He pulled against the loose panel and with a screech the whole section pulled away. Sssindy slithered out with a huge bulge in her middle.

"Thankssss!" she said. "That feelssss better!"

"I'll send you a bill for the damage to the back wall, David," Lusa said, "Once I get an estimate from Truck Stop Maintenance."

David sighed.

After they departed the Zoological Sanctuary, Racy, David, and Sssindy descended to the docking ring and walked (and slithered) antispinward until they arrived at the berth for her spaceship, *Never Back Down*. She flew a Xerxes Mark III. She opened the hatch and welcomed them inside.

"I didn't think there were any of these still flying," David said, looking around. "I thought my Mark VII was old."

"It's not the age: it's the lightyears, darling," Racy said, batting her eyes at David.

She showed Sssindy to the comms console and took her seat in the captain's chair.

"Truck Ssstop Ssspace Control, thisss isss *Never Back Down*. Captain Recklesssssss requessstsss immediate departure," Sssindy said.

A screen snapped red on the display.

"Sorry, *N.B.D.* A lien has been placed for your outstanding loan. They're demanding payment in full or they'll seize your ship."

"Oh, David?" Racy said, batting her eyes again. "I'm a little short until we do this job. Would you be a doll and front me the money? Just until we get paid?"

David looked at the red screen and his eyes bugged out.

"Why ... You could practically buy a new ship for that!"

"Oh, come on. It's not that much. And it's just for a few days.

David sighed. Again.

"Truck Stop Control. This is David. Add it to my tab for *Angels' Wings*." He pressed his thumb to the screen. There was a soft chime and the screen changed to green.

"Captain Reckless, you're cleared for departure."

Racy disengaged the spaceway and headed for the jump point with a light touch. Once they were underway, David got out his armor and took his time putting it on, making sure it was fitted and adjusted properly. As they went to jump, he stripped, cleaned, and checked the *Mottusuchi* from top to bottom, making certain it was in perfect working order.

•   •   •

Zaza heard a single guard approaching. She stood back from the door and centered herself. The door rattled and then opened.

"Come along," the guard said, his rail gun casually slung over his shoulder.

Zaza launched herself in a focused attack on his eyes, the only vulnerable part of his body not covered by his body armor. He fell back, blinded and screaming. She grabbed his railgun, spun the velocity setting to max and blew his head clean off, splattering the walls with blood and tissue. Then she loped down the hall, muzzle questing for targets.

She reached the door at the end of the hall, spun the bullet hardness to soft, and fired a round at the top of the door, which blasted a gigantic hole through the door. Then she spun the bullet hardness to max and, looking through the hole, took two clean shots, through the door at the stunned men standing inside who looked surprised at the neat holes through their chests before they collapsed to the ground. Bebe sat calmly in the chair while Zaza came through the door.

"Bebe tried to warn you," she said to them, in her singsong voice.

"Well done, Civilian," Zaza said. "But we're not out of this yet. Let's free the Gyarus!"

Zaza and Bebe returned to the corridor and began to open the doors to the other cells. They found the campers and Koguma and four other men as well. Koguma vomited when he saw the decapitated guard and associated mess, but Ĉiaki and Lin held him up and helped him follow along behind.

Zaza paused for a moment to address the strange men from the other cells.

"I don't know who you are," Zaza growled menacingly. "But if you do anything to threaten my Gyarus, I'll kill you."

"Yes, ma'am," one said.

As Zaza walked briskly to the front of the line to take the lead, Nadeŝko asked her as she went by, "Are you really twelve years old?"

"Sorry, Civilian," Zaza replied. "That's strictly need-to-know."

Zaza led everyone down the hallway toward the door where they'd come in. A guard poked his head around the corner and then ducked back around the corner. Zaza rolled her eyes, and fired through the wall. At max velocity, a hard bullet went through the walls like butter. It downed the guard and then kept going clean out of the compound. At the door, she poked her head out, and then pulled back as guards in the guard towers opened fire, and bullets kicked up the dust all around the entrance. She paused, daunted, with her terrified charges in tow.

•   •   •

David approached the facility keeping to the dappled shadows among the trunks. He had spotted two small sensors and disabled them at a distance with the pinbeam. But he moved cautiously in a wide circle around 500 meters away, observing, before approaching more closely. He looked around a large tree and noted men in body armor carrying railguns standing in guard towers surrounding the compound.

He was watching cautiously from the shadows when he heard the distinctive whine of a railgun firing. There was one report, a pause, then a loud report, and then two sharp reports. Two projectiles blasted through the walls of the compound and whistled past him, snapping leaves and twigs. The men in the guard towers became agitated and turned, looking down toward the compound. David raised the *Mottusuchi*, sighted and took careful note of the men. Suddenly there was a flurry of reports as the guards began shooting down toward the entrance. With the *Mottusuchi*, David fired nine times silently in rapid succession moving from target to target. The men, their spinal cords cut surgically at the base of the skull, dropped bonelessly. He waited. There was one more report as a tenth guard, not visible previously, fired at the entrance. David took a final shot and dropped him as well.

David observed, unsurprised — but with immense relief — as Zaza emerged from the compound leading the Angels and their associates. Moving slowly and keeping a careful watch, he cautiously approached them.

Zaza spotted him first.

"All present and accounted for, Top," she said casually, resting the railgun against her shoulder, her light tone belying her relief. "With four NRPs."

"Well done, Sergeant," he said. "You did well. But how is it you went active duty alone?"

"They took the devices from all the Gyarus at the camp, Top," she replied. "It seemed prudent that one of us be prepared."

"Good forethinking, Sergeant. Be careful! That kind of proactive attitude will get you promoted."

She grinned, cradling her railgun.

David approached the men Zaza had designated non-unit personnel.

"Opposition leader?"

One stepped forward.

"That's me. And these men are my bodyguards."

"I have transport for you," David said. "One moment."

He touched his headset.

"I have the package. We are go for extraction."

"Underssstood. You have the package. Ssstand by for extraction."

Moments later, the Xerxes Mark III streaked in and David led the four men inside. Then he turned and waved at the Angels.

"Enjoy the rest of your camping trip, Gyarus!"

"Bye, bye!" they called. "Bye, bye!"

With a roar, *Never Back Down* climbed up out of the forest and, in minutes, was headed for jump.

"What just happened?" Koguma said, holding his head.

"We need to get our Gyarus back to camp," Zaza said, slinging her railgun. "Let's move out!"

•　　•　　•

When the Gyarus arrived back at camp, Koguma and Zaza made a full report. The authorities were called and questioned everyone. They promised a full investigation. No-one admitted they had been aware of the illegal black site. But it also came out publicly that the Better Angels were there, which created huge enthusiasm among the campers — and the public at large. A few administrators questioned whether non-human biological androids should be allowed to participate in the camp, but those voices were quickly quashed and the Angels were welcomed into the camp with open arms. They let Zaza leave her soldier modules turned on, however, and she carried her railgun around to provide security for the Angels.

Zaza was on high alert when the Angels emerged from their tents wearing their swimsuits for swim lessons. Two men were on a nearby hilltop with high-powered telephoto lenses. They oohed and aahed as the Angels came into focus.

"Can you tell which one is which?" one asked.

"I think Bebe is the one wearing pink," the other replied.

"That's Tutu," Zaza said.

"Aah!" one yelled in surprise when he lifted his head and found himself looking down the barrel of a railgun.

"You've got 5 seconds to run before I open fire," Zaza said, emotionlessly. "And if I ever see you again, I'll shoot first."

The two men sprang to their feet. One tried to grab his expensive camera when Zaza put a bullet in it, knocking it out his hands, smashed beyond repair.

"Three seconds," she said.

They took to their heels and fled.

Zaza returned to the lake and stood by as the swim lessons continued. She stayed on high alert, scanning the environment tirelessly. Her eyes narrowed, when she caught a flash of light over the water. She raised her railgun and began to fire until she struck the tiny cameroid that was trying to spy on the Angels from overhead. Then she continued her wary and ceaseless vigil to keep the gawkers and paparazzi at bay.

On the last day, they held a graduation ceremony where all of the Gyarus were provided with official *Gyarakushīsukauto* leg warmers. The camp leader welcomed each Gyaru onto the stage where they pulled on their new legwarmers to the cheers of the campers.

As the ceremony wrapped up, everyone looked up as a grumbling roar grew in the sky and *Angels' Wings* descended into the camp.

David emerged from the cargo hatch and the Angels threw themselves onto him, hugging him and shrieking with excitement, while Zaza stood by stoically.

"I arranged for you to give the *Gyarakushīsukautos* a special performance."

He turned to Zaza.

"First Sergeant!"

"Yes, David!" she said, snapping proudly to attention.

"Come in and I'll have you stand down for the performance."

A half hour later, the Angels had changed into their pink-and-blue magical-girl costumes — but were also proudly wearing their *Gyarakushīsukauto* leg warmers. Zaza was still a bit shaky, but put on a brave face for her performance. The Better Angels emerged to deafening cheers and then the Gyarus really screamed to see Sssindy Serpent come out too.

"Are you ready, Gyarus?" Zaza called. "Let's get this show started!"

Sssindy tapped her tail on the stage and they sang and danced to a series of famous PuzzyCure songs. At sunset, they wrapped up the set with the obligate PuzzyCure camp song, *Baggler Call*:

Baggler Ichi, Baggler all!
Let's all do the Baggler Call!
Pss! Pss! Pss! Pss! Pss! Pss! Pss! Pss! Pss!
Baggler Ni, Baggler two!
Let's get stuck in Baggler glue!
Pss! Pss! Pss! Pss! Pss! Pss! Pss! Pss! Pss!
Baggler Shi! Baggler five!
Let's get stung in a Baggler hive!
Pss! Pss! Pss! Pss! Pss! Pss! Pss! Pss! Pss!
Baggler Go! Baggler six!
Let's all play some Baggler tricks!
Pss! Pss! Pss! Pss! Pss! Pss! Pss! Pss! Pss!
Baggler Shi Chi! Baggler eight!
Let's jump through the Baggler gate!
Pss! Pss! Pss! Pss! Pss! Pss! Pss! Pss! Pss!
Baggler Kyū! Baggler ten!
Let's do the Baggler Call again!

Finally, the Angels wrapped up the performance and, to deafening cheers, waving, they entered the cargo hatch. Zaza joined David in the bridge as he engaged the engines and *Angel's Wings* lifted off.

"Where to now?" she asked, innocently.

David sighed.

"I'm afraid this has been an expensive week. So I contacted Charlie. He's got some 'work' for us."

Zaza smiled.

"After our vacations, I think we're all ready for a little work."

THE BETTER ANGELS
AND
THE TOTALLY TOPSY-TURVY
TOURNAMENT

BEBE WALKED INTO DAVID'S STATEROOM scuffing her feet. "Bebe is bored," she said.

David was sitting at his desk digging through boxes of receipts and forms.

"I'm sorry, Bebe," he said. "I'm really busy right now."

Bebe went out scuffing her feet. Next she went to the galley and found Zaza.

"Bebe is bored," she said to Zaza.

Zaza was wearing rubber gloves trying to clean a stubborn stain off the counter.

"I can't play right now, Bebe," she said. "Maybe later."

Bebe wandered aimlessly through *Angels' Wings*. She looked for Sssindy and then remembered that she'd been offered a huge sum of credits to deal with another nest of magarats somewhere deep in the Truck Stop at the Center of the Galaxy. Bebe sighed.

The buzzer rang at the hatch for *Angels' Wings*.

David called, "Can someone get that? I'm trying to get the taxes done."

"My hands are dirty because I'm cleaning up a mess," Zaza said. "Can someone else go?"

"We're watching a show!" Sisi called. "It's the exciting part!"

"Bebe can go!" Bebe shrieked, excitedly, running out to the hatch. She triggered it but there was no-one there. She looked back and forth, up and down the Docking Ring of the Truck Stop, but could see no-one. But then she looked down and found a package sitting just outside the spaceway. She picked it up and carried it in.

"Bebe has a package," she called.

"Who's it for?" David called back.

Bebe looked at the label.

"Bebe doesn't know this name," she said. "Someone named … Gaetz?"

"Ugh!" shouted David and all of the Angels simultaneously. "Throw it in the recycler!"

"Bebe wants to see what it is first!" she said.

Bebe carried the box back to her stateroom and opened it. Inside the packaging was another box. It had a picture of a huge soldier on it wearing body armor and carrying a Corona-14. They were chomping on a big cigar and standing on top of a giant pile of dead bodies in a fantastic scene of carnage. The label on the box said, "*Moshimoshi SutāyUnibāsu*".

"Awesome!" Bebe whispered. She found a packing sheet that indicated this was a warranty replacement for something that had been returned more than a year ago.

She opened the box and looked inside. There was a kind of headset and two hand-held controllers. An information sheet showed how to put the headset on and hold the controllers. After putting them on, she pressed the button and she was transported to a bare metal room with a mirror and was looking at a hairy, hugely-muscled, nearly-naked man in the mirror. Panicked, she quickly turned the power off and was back in her room. Breathing deeply, she turned the power on again and, once more, she was in the bare metal room looking at the figure in the mirror. When she raised an arm, he raised an arm. She trotted in place and he trotted in place. She grinned and he made a terrifying grimace at the mirror and chomped his cigar.

"Let's get this show on the road," he growled.

A series of prompts and controls appeared on the wall that she realized she could use to adjust her avatar. She spent a half hour just playing with options: There were a huge range of choices including NeoBoxers and 'pedes. Finally, she decided to make herself look like herself. She made herself a small female character wearing pink-and-blue form-fitting body armor with a short skirt and a helmet with cat ears. Then she clicked the blinking start icon.

She appeared in a ruined city under a dark, stormy sky. There were shattered buildings and overturned vehicles. Bullets started to whine past her, so she ran around a corner and was instantly cut down by a blast from a Corona-14. She floated above her body for a moment, hearing the sounds of battle fade, and then she returned to the loading room. She giggled.

"Bebe thinks this is amazing!" she breathed. And pressed Start again.

•   •   •

Zaza called everyone for lunch, but Bebe didn't come. After lunch, Zaza tracked her down in her room, standing in the middle with a funny headset on, turning in circles making shooting gestures.

"Bebe," she said.

Bebe made no response.

"Bebe!" she said louder.

Still no response.

"BEBE!" she yelled.

Bebe spun and then looked at Zaza.

"What?"

"Lunch. You missed lunch."

"Lunch!" Bebe shrieked. "Bebe is STARVING!"

She ran lightly down to the galley where a Fun Meal had been prepared for her — now cold. She stood at the counter, shook out the bag and started munching on the cold sandwich.

"What's that ... thing?" Zaza asked, pointing.

"Oh! It's a fun game! Bebe loves it! Do you want to try it?" She helped Zaza put it on.

"You can play with Bebe's character to see what it's like."

While Bebe ate her Fun Meal, she watched Zaza turn in circles and gesticulate.

"I died," she said.

"It happens," Bebe said, around a mouthful of sandwich.

"This is fun," Zaza said, starting it up again.

"Bebe knows, right?

"Your rank seems pretty low at 8,456,124," Zaza observed.

"It was lower than a billion when Bebe started," Bebe said, defensively. "Bebe thinks you need a team if you want to get a high score."

"A team … Can we get more headsets?"

"Bebe doesn't know!"

"Let's ask Lala if we can replicate them!"

After Bebe finished gobbling her Fun Meal, she and Zaza found Lala dozing in the lounge. Bebe pulled on her sleeve and she yawned and took a look at the device.

"Sure," she said, rubbing her eyes. "We can replicate that."

"Yay!" Bebe said, jumping up and down with excitement

"Why did Gaetz need to get a replacement, then?" Zaza asked.

"Probably because it was broken," Lala replied. "If you replicate something that's broken, it's still broken."

Lala carried the device to the replicator and ran it through the analyzer.

"How many do you want?"

"Let's make enough for everyone!" Zaza said.

A half hour later, Zaza called the Angels back to Hold One and distributed the game sets.

"What's this? What are we doing?"

"Bebe found this game and it's really fun," Zaza explained. Bebe beamed to be credited.

"Before we start," Zaza said. "It says we need to name our team. What shall we call ourselves?"

"Bebe thinks we should be the Avenging Angels!"

Everyone concurred and so Zaza entered the name in the tournament roster.

Bebe led them through the sign-in process and, within minutes, they were all in-world together: A squad of nine, identical soldiers wearing pink-and-blue body armor and helmets with cat ears.

"I'll go this way?" Sisi said.

"What's up there?" Mumu said.

"Which weapon should I use?" asked Tutu.

"We need to work together!" Zaza said.

"Aaah!" screamed Nene as she was gunned down.

"Where do we go to ..." Popo started to say when an *Ublyudok* from a distant shooter took her down.

"Bebe says to listen to Zaza!"

After a few more tries, they got organized and started to climb the rankings. By dinner time, they had reached the thousands, but their progress had slowed to a standstill. They decided to take a break for dinner.

"What would you like for dinner?" Zaza called to David.

"I'm almost done!" he called back. "Go ahead without me!"

"Sounds like Fun Meals again!" Zaza said, rubbing her hands.

Lala ran the replicator and generated Fun Meals for everyone. Then the Angels stood around in the galley and wolfed them, eager to get back and play the game some more.

As they trotted back to Hold One, Bebe said, "Bebe wants someone to give her orders."

"That's it!" Zaza said. She pulled out her device and made a quick adjustment. The Angels watched as her expression and body language changed. "Lock and load, Recruits!" she barked. They pulled out their devices and followed suit. Then they put on the headsets and logged in.

"Bebe is jacked up and good to go!" growled Bebe.

"Sisi! Take Lala and Nene to the rooftop. Tutu! Take Mumu and Popo to the left. Bebe and Rara — you're with me!"

"Yes, Sarge!" they shouted.

With the soldier modules, their teamwork was impeccable. Their opponents didn't stand a chance and, in battle after battle, they climbed the rankings until they were number 2. Then they were fought to a standstill by the top ranked team and had to take a draw.

"We need the Master Sergeant!" Zaza said. The Angels all ran to David's stateroom.

"Master Sergeant! Master Sergeant!" they all shrieked. "Lock and load! It's an emergency!"

David was poised with his finger over the screen.

"I just need to check one more thing," he said. "Then I'll ..."

"No! No! No!" they all squealed, pulling at his clothes. "Now! Now! Now!"

"Is it really that serious?"

"Bebe thinks it's the most important thing in the galaxy!" Bebe said, with a grave expression.

David sighed and let himself be dragged into Hold One and allowed the Angels to fit him with a headset and controllers. He pulled out his device and made the necessary adjustments.

"Jacked up and good to go," he growled. And then he logged into the environment. He saw the name of the team and his eye twitched.

When the Angels appeared in the shattered city, they found themselves aligned with a new player using the default avatar: a hugely muscled, hairy man wearing nothing but a loincloth and chomping a cigar.

"Tutu! Take your squad and scout," he barked. "Sisi, your team is rearguard. Zaza! Lead your team up that tower and cover us with the *Ublyudok*s."

"Aye, aye, Top!" they shouted.

They took up their positions and, when Tutu's squad engaged with the enemy, they were perfectly positioned. David charged forward with a *Mottusuchi* in one hand and an *Ublyudok* in the other and fired both simultaneously with deadly accuracy.

A squad of the enemy trying to sneak around behind was dispatched by Sisi's team deployed at their flank. They took down the members of the opposing team one after another until just one was left. He tried to run but Bebe, at long range, opened fire with an *Ublyudok*. It made a screaming report and blasted him. His avatar dropped.

"We did it! We did it!" they all shrieked watching their rank roll over to number 1. Then the environment turned red and logged them out with a big flashing warning message, "AVENGING ANGELS BANNED FOR AIMBOTTING."

The Angels stood stunned for several seconds then began to stamp and howl with fury.

"Not fair!" Bebe shouted. "Bebe is mad!"

"We should go to the company headquarters on Volpex," Sisi said. "Take the fight to them!"

"Go! Go! Go!" Lala said.

"We gotta move!" Nene said.

"Gimme something to shoot!" Tutu said.

"Master Sergeant!" Zaza barked. "The troop suggests setting coordinates to Volpex!"

David rolled his eyes and said, "Stand down, Angels."

As one, they collapsed to the floor shaking violently from withdrawal from the soldier modules.

David carried them, one by one, to their beds and tucked them in.

"I'm sorry, David," Zaza said, still trembling as he carried her last to her bed. "I guess we got carried away over the game."

"Oh, Angel. Never change," he said, then grinned malevolently. "Now let me finally go finish the taxes, while I'm in the right frame of mind."

THE BETTER ANGELS AND THE ABSOLUTELY APROPOS ARRANGEMENT

"REPORTING LIVE FROM TELLUS, this is Mandy Fourteen," said a syrupy voice as the Angels strutted between the velvet ropes amid screams of excitement. Zaza spotted the reporter standing at the edge — a young blond woman with a small, hovering cameroid.

After their performance, the Better Angels were returning to *Angels' Wings* along the red carpet, gauntleted by their screaming fans. The Angels were by themselves on this tour — Sssindy wasn't with them this time. She had gotten desperate pleas from several groups on the Truck Stop that were being overrun with magarats, and had stayed behind to try to help.

"The Better Angels have once again incomprehensibly wowed an audience with their programmed singing and dancing," Mandy Fourteen continued, in a scathing tone.

Zaza heard the reporter and didn't react, but noticed when Bebe stiffened. Before she could be provoked into saying anything impolitic, Zaza turned to the reporter.

"Perhaps your viewers would like to see us rehearse tomorrow."

The cameroid turned toward the Angels who struck a pose as the crowd went wild.

"I'll be there," Mandy said with a predatory smile.

•　　•　　•

"Mandy Fourteen has been putting the worst possible spin on everything since the beginning," David said. "She may just use this visit to gather more ammunition."

"I hear what you're saying," Zaza said. "But maybe we can change her mind."

The hatch buzzed and Zaza went to the spaceway and opened it. Mandy Fourteen had brought three cameroids that floated in around her.

"Welcome to *Angels' Wings!*" Zaza said, with a gracious bow.

"Thank you for inviting me," Mandy said. "I'm rather surprised, since I had requested interviews several times previously."

Zaza smiled.

"Won't you come in? Please follow me to Hold One where we hold our daily rehearsals."

Zaza led the reporter through the starship.

"Why is it called 'Hold One'?" Mandy asked, as one cameroid focused on her and another on Zaza.

"*Angels' Wings* was originally a military troop transport ..."

"I hear rumors that it still sometimes serves as that," Mandy interrupted.

Zaza ignored her and continued. "But it was converted to a freighter and, after we bought it, the largest cargo hold was converted to our dance studio."

They arrived in Hold One where the rest of the Angels were wearing comfortable, identical, pink-and-blue sweats and watching a performance showing on a wall-sized display.

"We're getting ready for a new show," Zaza explained. "We're going to perform at a dozen venues on planets where it's summertime. So we're developing a new show of summertime music."

"So what are we looking at?"

"This is an original PuzzyCure recording of *Sassy Summer.*"

"And you're just programmed to copy this performance?"

Zaza found herself starting to lose patience with the constant needling, but intentionally calmed herself down and responded carefully.

"Our performances are not programmed. Nor are we programmed to copy performances. It's true that our programming allows us to easily learn a performance by watching it. But we watch multiple interpretations by different groups when developing our routines."

"So you can copy those performances?"

"Bebe doesn't just copy!" Bebe shouted.

Two of the cameroids swung around and focused on Bebe. She drew herself up and put her hands on her hips.

"Bebe watches the other dances, but her moves are her own!"

"But you're limited by your programming — you're only programmed to copy singing and dancing. You can't really do anything else."

"Bebe can do anything!" Bebe screamed.

"I have an idea!" Mandy said, with an ingenuous smile. "There's an *ikebana* competition happening next week on the Truck Stop at the Center of the Galaxy. Why don't the Better Angels participate and show us your so-called creativity. Show us how you can do anything!"

"Bebe will!" Bebe snarled. "And Bebe will win!"

After Mandy Fourteen had left, Bebe asked, "What's *ikebana*?"

The Angels conferred with David. He sighed.

"*Ikebana* is flower arranging. It's complicated and requires a lot of specialized knowledge. It's not something anyone can master in a week. And I don't have any programming modules for it."

The Angels looked at one another glumly.

"But Bebe wants to win ..." Bebe said, plaintively.

"Let's call Charles," David said. "Maybe he will have some ideas."

•   •   •

The next day, after they had returned to the Truck Stop, there was a buzz at the hatch of *Angels' Wings*.

"I'll get it!" Bebe shrieked and ran to the hatch.

When she opened the hatch, a small, elderly man was there. He wore a black suit with a battered fedora. He bowed slightly.

"Pardon me for disturbing you," he said. "Is David here?

"David!" Bebe screamed, running toward the bridge. The man cringed and covered his ears.

David walked out briskly.

"I'm sorry," David said. "The Angels are always exuberant. Welcome to *Angels' Wings!*"

"My name is Hachi. Hachi Ikatteiru. Charles Downsend asked me to teach your girls *Ikebana*, the gentle art of flower arranging."

"Thank you for coming, Mr. Ikatteiru. Let me introduce you to the Angels."

David led Mr. Ikatteiru back to Hold One where the Angels were busy rehearsing. When they came in, the Angels ran over shrieking and danced in circles around them both, jumping up and down. Mr. Ikatteiru's expression hardened.

"This behavior is most unseemly," he said, sharply. "The art of *ikebana* must be joyful, but also solemn and dignified. I can't teach you if you behave thus."

Zaza hushed the Angels and then turned and bowed. The Angels all assumed seiza position before him.

"Please teach us, *Sensei!*" they all said together.

Mollified, he addressed them.

"The ancient art of *ikebana* has three principles: harmony, balance, and minimalism. But a key goal is to bring a fresh approach, which requires one to know what's been done and to innovate new forms of presentation. Let me show you."

He brought up a series of photographs on their display wall and continued explaining the history and philosophy of ikebana, supplemented with examples of previous prize-winning arrangements. The Angels paid attention carefully, though they began to squirm after a while.

Then the hatch buzzed again and, hearing a click-click-click, the Angels all sprang to their feet and ran over shrieking. "Cap'n Tau! Cap'n Tau!"

He leapt among them jumping up and licking their faces while they giggled happily.

"Cap'n Tau! You have to try too!"

Tau barked and they all said, "*Ikebana!*"

"Bebe is learning to make flower arrangements!" Bebe said. "You have to enter the competition too!"

"A dog?" Mr. Ikatteiru said, scornfully. "You think a dog can learn *Ikebana*?"

"He's not *just* a dog," David explained. "This is a NeoBoxer."

Tau barked.

"Well, yes ..." Mr. Ikatteiru said. "That's true."

Tau barked again.

"Yes, yes, of course. That's a good point too. I withdraw my remark."

Then the hatch buzzed again and the Angels looked up when David entered, leading a long line of deliveroids carrying boxes and baskets.

"Ah! Right on time!" Mr Ikatteiru said. "Mr. Downsend also arranged for this delivery of flowers, containers, and other materials that you can use to construct your arrangements. Now, let's get started."

The Angels sprang to their feet and, shrieking, began to run around inspecting all of the different kinds of colorful flowers and containers. Mr. Ikatteiru had a pained expression on face watching the Angels jump up and down with excitement, but eventually relaxed and walked among the Angels as they began trying to make flower arrangements. He offered helpful suggestions and guidance.

"Ah! You don't want any flowers to stand straight up. Pitch them at 10 degrees," he said to Tutu.

"No, no, no! You don't want the flowers all at the same level," he said to Sisi. "Cut one shorter and another shorter still."

"Try not to have even numbers of blossoms or stems," he said to Mumu. "Have one or three or five."

"Don't put it right at the center," he said to Bebe. "Have it offset. Aim for asymmetry and a sense of movement."

Mr. Ikatteiru went over to where Tau was working and looked at his arrangement.

"This is ... quite good. Are you sure you've never done this before? No? Amazing!"

After he had finished his arrangement, Captain Tau also circulated, inspecting the Angels' arrangements. He looked at Bebe's and barked.

"Ooh! Bebe likes that idea!" Bebe said, sticking her tongue out to concentrate on what she was doing. "Bebe will try!"

"And what's on this rack?" Zaza asked, pointing at something a deliveroid had brought that was over to the side.

"Ah! Mr. Downsend wanted you to be properly attired for the event. There is a kimono for each of you. I will teach you how to tie the obi."

•   •   •

On the day of the event, the Angels filed into the large event space in the Blue Sector of the Truck Stop at the Center of the Galaxy where the *Ikebana* competition was being held. They walked solemnly in a row, each wearing a colorful kimono, each with a different, brilliant pattern: sakura blossoms, nebulas, chrysanthemums, dragonflies, camelias, galaxies, cranes, and other traditional patterns.

In the huge room, there were dozens of long tables. The Angels placed their entries along with nearly a hundred other arrangements that had been submitted for judging.

"Hi, Sssweetiesss," Sssindy said, slithering up from behind.

"Sssindy! Sssindy!" the Angels shrieked, until they remembered to tamp down their enthusiasm and act with decorum.

"We're all very pleased to see you, Miss Serpent," Zaza said, bowing.

Amid crowds of spectators, five judges — three women and two men — went through the space and carefully considered each one. The first entry was by a 5-year-old girl.

"Cerulean Dreams by Molly Moon," read a judge.

Her arrangement was contained in a pretty blue vase and had blossoms from two house plants she had collected together. The judges studied it seriously, made notations on their scoring sheet, and then moved to the next one.

The head judge, a white-haired, older man, studied each entry and recorded his observations as he tried to fairly assess them. It was tedious to participate in an amateur competition like this. So many of the presentations were trite, poorly conceived, and poorly executed. He noticed some excitement toward one side of the room and realized that a journalist was there with hovering cameroids to cover the event.

"This is Mandy Fourteen coming to you live from the Truck Stop *Ikebana* Competition. Today we're here to see how well — if at all — the Better Angels can be programmed to arrange flowers."

The judge looked around and spotted the famous Better Angels. They were in a small group, clustered together, surrounded by fans. They were leading a man through their entries, excitedly showing him what they'd made. The judge was charmed, watching. As they came to each entry, one of the Angels would explain her entry, and the others would all strike a pose around her.

The judges finished with one entry and trudged to the next. Then they recoiled when they were assailed by a shocking odor. Flies buzzed above a container with what appeared, at first glance, to be a pile of stinking offal. Upon closer inspection, they discovered it was an artistically arranged set of half-digested small-animal corpses that appeared to have been regurgitated.

"Magarat Mayhem by Sssindy Serpent?" one of the female judges read, wrinkling her nose with disgust. Then she howled with horror when one of the corpses, which wasn't quite dead, began to stir, thrashing weakly in the container.

"Disqualified!" the judges all shouted. They called for security to remove the arrangement and Sssindy was expelled from the competition.

After the unpleasant excitement, the head judge returned to the dreary task, looking at one tiresome entry after another. Periodically, he let his eyes drift back to the Angels, in high spirits, going to each of their arrangements. And at each one they would array themselves around the Angel describing her creation and take a pose. Then it struck him like lightning. The Angels, in their colorful kimonos, were like flowers themselves. And they were arranging themselves! And their arrangements were perfect!

"Look! Look! Look!" he hissed to the other judges.

"What?" said one.

"Look! *Ikebana*! Have you ever seen such harmony? Such balance?"

A woman judge gasped when she saw it too. Spellbound, they

watched the Angels until they completed their circuit. Then the judges all conferred with one another and reached consensus.

"Well, it doesn't look like the Angels' programming will win them any prizes today," Mandy Fourteen said, as she reviewed some of the scores the Angels' flower arrangements had received. "Androids just can't be programmed for true artistic ability."

"Attention please! We're ready to announce the winners," the judge said. The audience quieted and everyone paid attention.

"It was very hard to choose," he said. "All of the contestants have offered beautiful arrangements upholding the highest principles of *ikebana*.

"Third place is awarded to Bebe for her innovative arrangement 'Lollipop Flower and Bubblegum Phlox'."

The Angels all cheered and struck a pose around Bebe, who blushed and shuffled her feet. Mandy Fourteen looked like she'd been slapped.

"Second place goes to Tau, for his arrangement 'Sanctuary Bamboo' which demonstrated a unique, interesting, minimalistic approach."

Tau whirled in circles as the Angels cheered him on enthusiastically.

"And finally, before we announce the winner, let me explain something about the true spirit of *ikebana*," the judge continued. "Although we think of it as flower arranging, its philosophy of movement, harmony, and balance can be applied to anything — even to sticks or rocks or fish bones. Or people.

"By unanimous decision, we award the *ikebana* first prize to the Better Angels for the arrangement of themselves at each of the flower arrangements. All of us were in awe of their movement, harmony, balance — and their fresh approach. We salute their creativity and dedication to their craft."

The Angels shrieked with excitement and danced in a circle jumping up and down. The crowd applauded and whistled with appreciation. Mandy Fourteen, with a sour expression, started to turn away, but Bebe ran to her.

"Bebe wants to thank you!" she said. "Bebe had a lot of fun and learned a lot!" Then she pointed and shrieked, "WHAT IS THAT?"

Mandy's cameroids all swung to record what she was pointing at when Bebe stepped up close to Mandy. Mandy instinctively went to take a step back and bumped into Tau who had moved to just behind her knees. She toppled over backward and her breath huffed out as she fell hard. Her cameroids swung back to record her as she struggled, red-faced, to get back to her feet.

"Bebe says to watch where you're going!" Bebe laughed, as she ran back to the rest of the Angels.

THE BETTER ANGELS
AND
THE PERSISTENT PROPOSALS OF
PRINCE PHILIP

F OR THREE SHOWS, on three different worlds, the Better Angels noticed a young man occupying the same seat in the front row. When they arrived at the next world, Chevalio, trumpets sounded when they came through the spaceway. The young man was standing at the hatch wearing a white uniform, surrounded by an entourage of many officials.

"Miss Popo?" he said.

"Yes?" Popo said, coming forward.

"I am Prince Philip of Chevalio and I would like to request your hand in marriage as my princess."

"No," Popo said. And then the Angels swept on as a group past Prince Philip, between the velvet ropes, to the venue where they delivered their performance.

Several days later, upon returning to the Truck Stop at the Center of the Galaxy, the Better Angels received special handwritten invitations to attend a fancy-dress ball paid for by an anonymous benefactor. They were promised elegant, non-replicated, custom-fitted, designer gowns. The Angels were ecstatic.

"Bebe can't wait!" Bebe said.

"It sounds like a trap," David said.

When they arrived at the Delphian Ballroom, they were led off into a fitting room where they were presented with floor-length gowns of lace with tiers of ruffles. Attendants helped them dress, apply make-up, and fix their hair.

When they emerged, Popo found herself face-to-face with Prince Philip who was dressed in a stylish tuxedo of the latest fashion.

"You are the true belle of the ball," he murmured to Popo. "Will you marry me?"

"No," Popo said.

Several weeks later, the Better Angels were in a gigantic stadium, wrapping up a 12-planet tour of summertime music. The audience rose to their feet cheering as the music came to a shattering crescendo and the Angels struck their final pose. Then every single audience member held up either a white or black placard so that the entire stadium displayed one gigantic message: "MISS POPO: WILL YOU MARRY ME?"

Prince Philip knelt in the front row and held up a case with a sparkling ring.

"No," Popo said.

But then everyone gasped when Popo visibly blushed.

A week later, the Better Angels were on a benefit run to support children's education on Beltran-2. It was hot and the Angels sweated, running through streets lined with fans and supporters.

When they reached the hydration station, volunteers were lined up offering cups with water. But Popo noticed that her volunteer was Prince Philip who held up an ornate golden chalice encrusted with gems.

"When we're married, you could drink from this every day," he said. "Wouldn't you like that?"

"No," Popo said and continued on her run.

A few days later, when the Better Angels finished their afternoon performance on Celtron-4, they returned to *Angels' Wings* just as night was falling.

"I know a place not far from here where there's something special to see," David said. "Let me take you there."

He laid in a course and they flew east to a tiny, rocky island far out in a vast ocean.

The Angels exited and looked up at the heavens. It was midnight on the island and the stars twinkled brilliantly against a sky that was absolutely black from horizon to horizon.

"Ooh!" they all gasped.

Then an armada of tiny pyrotechnicoids lit up overhead and spelled out in giant glowing letters across the sky, "MISS POPO: PLEASE MARRY ME!"

"No!" she screamed.

•　　•　　•

Angels' Wings docked at Diplomacy Prime, a giant asteroid near the center of the galaxy dedicated to resolving disputes among the federated planets.

Popo strode forward backed by David and the Better Angels. They arrived at the Grand Council Chamber and opened the door at the same time that Prince Philip arrived at the other side. They advanced and met in the middle.

"You have now proposed many times and been rejected," Popo said. "Are you ever going to stop proposing to me?"

"No," Prince Philip said.

Even after much discussion, the mediators were unable to resolve their differences. And so they departed, leaving from opposite sides of the Grand Council Chamber. The Better Angels were most of the way back to *Angels' Wings*, when Prince Philip came running from behind.

"Wait, Miss Popo! Wait!"

The Angels all turned and waited as he arrived breathlessly, panting, and pulled out his device.

"Could I at least get your contact info?" he asked.

"No," Popo said.

•　　•　　•

Prince Philip walked briskly down the Docking Ring at the Truck Stop at the Center of the Galaxy headed toward *Angels' Wings*.

"Today," he thought, confidently. "Today's the day she'll finally say 'yes.'" But when he saw the spaceway to *Angels' Wings*, he became consumed with doubt and, in the end, he lost his nerve and just kept walking. Eventually, he took the elevator up and went into the Zoological Sanctuary to think. He wandered aimlessly for a while and then, depressed, he sat on a bench. He was sitting there with his head in his hands when Tau approached.

Tau sat next to him and ruffed.

"Hmm? Yeah," Prince Philip said. "I'm not having a good day." He sighed. "Or a good week."

Tau nudged him with his muzzle.

"Oh. I keep proposing to my beloved, but she keeps saying 'no.' Maybe I should just give up."

Tau ruffed again.

"You say that," Philip said miserably. "But do you really think there's any hope?"

Tau sprang to his feet and barked.

"Really? You think it's just that I'm rushing things? What do you think I should do?"

Tau ruffed again and Prince Philip leapt to his feet.

"That's a great idea! I'll do it!"

•   •   •

The hatch chimed on *Angels' Wings* and Bebe ran for the hatch shrieking, "I'll get it!"

She triggered the hatch and it opened to reveal Prince Philip standing outside. He bowed respectfully.

"Is Miss Popo in?"

"Popo!" Bebe screamed running back toward the lounge.

Philip waited at the hatch and a few moments later, Popo arrived. When she saw who it was, she opened her mouth to say, 'No,' but Philip spoke first.

"I brought you these, Miss Popo." He offered her a bouquet of rather prosaic flowers. "They said I could pick them myself at the Zoological Sanctuary."

"Thank you," she said, accepting the bouquet. She smelled them and smiled.

"I also wanted to apologize for trying to rush things so much. I talked to ... someone who said that maybe it's too soon to ask you to marry."

"Oh, Philip," she said. "It's not too soon. It's just impossible. I'm not ever going to marry you."

"Well, even if you won't marry me, would you go on a date with me?" Prince Philip stood up straight and waited anxiously for Popo to reply.

Popo opened her mouth to say, 'no,' but then closed it again and thought for a moment. All the other Angels were staying back, but jostling each other trying to hear and see what was going on.

"Yes," said Popo.

"Ooooh!" said all the Angels.

"Great!" said Philip, as Popo blushed. "Can I pick you up around 19:00?"

"I'll be ready," she said.

•   •   •

At the appointed hour, Prince Philip called again and buzzed at the spaceway. Popo came herself and opened the hatch. He was turned out in his impeccable white uniform. His eyes widened as he saw she was wearing casual clothes: a pink cashmere sweater, a blue sailor skirt — short but not too short — and comfortable shoes. Philip offered his arm and Popo took it.

"I know just the place," he said.

They walked together to the elevators and rode up to the Main Ring. As they strolled, Popo asked, "So why me?"

"What?" Prince Philip asked, genuinely puzzled. "Because you're you! You're the only one for me."

"Well, but let me ask you this," Popo said. She stopped by a left-over Better Angels poster still on the wall from a recent benefit they had done. It showed a group picture of the Angels standing together in costume. "Tell me! Which one is me?" she demanded.

"This one," he said, picking her out instantly from among the others.

She looked at him, shocked.

"Well, I have to admit," he said. "I can't always tell all of the others apart." He gestured at the image again. "This one is Bebe. And this one is Zaza. And I'm pretty sure that's Sisi. But I have a hard time telling Lala, Mumu, Nene, Rara, and Tutu apart. But I can *always* recognize you. Of course I can!"

Popo tapped her lips with surprise. And then smiled.

Prince Philip offered his arm again and they walked a short distance spinward to The Restaurant. Prince Philip was recognized and they were promptly whisked away to a quiet, out-of-the way table.

"What would you recommend?" Popo asked, after studying the menu.

"I understand they can make a pretty good Fun Meal," he said. She looked over at him and his eyes twinkled. She grinned back.

"You know so much about me," she said. "But I don't know anything about you."

"I thought you'd never ask!" he laughed. And, after a moment, she joined in too.

•   •   •

After dinner, he escorted her out of the restaurant and they started walking back toward *Angels' Wings*.

"I wanted to be sure to get you back on time," he said. "So I took the liberty of getting you a dessert you can take with you." He handed her a lollipop.

She accepted it with an expression of wonder.

"How did you know?"

He just smiled knowingly.

Popo and Prince Philip strolled back to *Angels' Wings* and arrived just as 22:00 was striking. She triggered the hatch and entered, then turned to face him. *Angels' Wings* was silent, as the other Angels were already in bed, asleep.

"Thank you for a lovely evening," she said. "Everything was perfect and I had a very nice time."

"You're welcome," he said. "It's a night I will remember and cherish for the rest of my life."

They paused, awkwardly, for a moment, then Prince Philip smiled wryly and said, "Now will you marry me?" Then grinned, eyes sparkling.

Popo smiled. Then she stepped forward, stretched up on her toes, and gave him a kiss on the cheek. Then she stepped back.

"No," she said.

He waved and turned to go, then turned back.

"You know," he said. "Some people just can't take no for an answer."

THE BETTER ANGELS
AND
THE GIDDY GENIAL GAG

AFTER *ANGELS' WINGS* DETACHED from the Truck Stop and was headed toward the jump point, the Better Angels came out to the bridge in a mob and started pulling on David's clothes and hands.

"David! David! David!" they said.

"What? What? What?" he replied.

"Charades! We want to play charades!"

"Charades?" David asked, wrinkling up his nose. "Can't you just play that yourselves?"

"No! No! No!," they pleaded. "You have to play too! Please?"

"Oh, alright ..." He locked the console and followed them back to the lounge and they all took seats, the Angels sprawling out on the couches and cushions on the floor.

"Who's going to go first?" he asked.

The Angels all shrugged and looked at one another. David rolled his eyes.

"How about this: Let's go in reverse alphabetical order." Everyone looked at Zaza. She thought for a moment then stood up and held up three fingers, then one.

"Um ... Three words," said David. "First word."

Zaza indicated herself.

"I," David said.

Zaza clapped her hands and the Angels all cheered. Then Zaza held up three fingers.

"Third word," David said.

Zaza pointed at David.

"Me. No, you!"

Zaza clapped again. Then the Angels all started holding their breath. Zaza held up two fingers and then she made a heart symbol by holding her hands together.

"Hands? Heart?" David began, then he said, "No! It's 'love'! I love you!"

"Oooooh!" all of the Angels cried out together.

Zaza blushed coquettishly and looked down, shifting from foot to foot with her hands clasped behind her back.

Then all the Angels began to chant, "David and Zaza, sittin' in a tree, K-I-S-S-I-N-G ..."

David got up and silently stalked out.

THE BETTER ANGELS
AND
THE PARABLE OF
THE PRODIGAL PIRATE

THE BETTER ANGELS CREPT FORWARD through the shadows of the darkened corridors of Tenable-5, a space station near a lucrative asteroid mining region. They had forced an airlock, thanks to an ingenious device that David had, which overwhelmed the security and prevented it from alerting the central system. From around a corner, they could hear a man ranting. Zaza, Bebe, and Rara got down on their bellies and slithered forward, cradling railguns and keeping to the shadows while the others hung back.

"Ye've got 30 minutes!" the man bellowed. "If the funds are not transferred by then, we start spacing the captives." He grabbed a young woman by the shirt. "Let's start with ye! What's yer name?"

"Mari Timdale," she whimpered.

"Unless ya want Mari Timdale to come to a gruesome end, ye'll have the credits transferred in just … 28 minutes."

"We need more time!" a voice said desperately, over the speaker. "We don't have access to those kinds of funds on such short notice!"

"Tsk! Well, if Mari isn't worth saving, there's plenty more where she came from!" the man continued.

Zaza, in the lead, peeked around the corner. There were four men carrying railguns standing in the corners of the room and another man with a Corona-18 — a veritable cannon compared with the Corona-14. And, finally, in the middle, a strangely-dressed older man with a gray beard who appeared unarmed. He wore odd striped, baggy trousers tied with a yellow sash, a loose, bright-red silk shirt, and a bandana tied over his bald head.

Bebe and Rara slithered up next to Zaza while the other Angels hung back waiting for the command.

"Go!" David whispered in their earpieces. Zaza, Bebe, and Rara took simultaneous shots from their positions and landed headshots on two of the men with railguns and the one with the Corona-18. While the other two were turning toward the threat, Sisi and Tutu sprang around the corner and gunned them down.

The oddly-dressed man took to his heels as David stepped forward. The man reached a hatch and looked back for a moment.

"Hold your fire," David said to the Angels.

"Give me regards to Charlie, matey!" the man cried and slammed the hatch shut.

Zaza looked at David who stared impassively at the door. David shook his head and the moment passed.

The captives were exceedingly grateful and thanked David and the Angels over and over for rescuing them from the madman who was holding them for ransom. Captain Tau, who was piloting *Angel's Wings* docked with the space station and they trooped back across.

Later, after they'd stood down and recovered from the after effects of turning off their soldier modules, Zaza ran out to the bridge in her nightgown.

"David," she said, putting her little hands on his arm. "Would you please tell us a bedtime story?"

David followed her back to the lounge where all of the Angels were in their nightgowns with pillows and blankets waiting patiently for a story.

"What kind of story would you like tonight?"

"Tell us a story about a princess," Lala said.

"Tell Bebe a story about a banana!" Bebe said. The other Angels looked at her askance.

"Tell us a story about a *pirate*," Zaza said. David looked at her. She smiled disarmingly, and settled in. David shook his head, sighed, and began to speak.

•　　•　　•

There was once a military non-human biological android. He was replicated into an army at war and began as a private, as most of you did. Where and when doesn't really matter. But, over the time of the war, he rose through the ranks and eventually became a Master Sergeant.

But then his side in the war lost. The war came to a sudden end and there was no longer any call for soldiers. The humans went back to their lives, but the androids were sold off. Some ended up doing asteroid mining — hard, dangerous, unforgiving work. Some were sold to gladiator pits, to fight for human entertainment.

Due to my ... his ... rank, the price was rather high and so he was among the last to be sold. He was the last one in the holding cell when an odd man came in. He had a red beard and was strangely dressed, wearing colorful baggy clothes. And he was really drunk.

"I need me some hearty crew," he said, striking a pose in front of the bars.

"Are you talking to me?" the android said.

"Aye, matey!" the man said. "And I'll thank ye to address me as CAP'N!"

The android looked at the weirdo and said, "Yes, Captain."

"Now that'sh what I'm talkin' 'bout!" he slurred.

He paid the exorbitant fee and received the authorization code to the android. He directed the android to follow him back to his starship, the *Akahata*. There, he typed a set of coordinates into the console and, without a word, went to his bunk, threw himself down, and went to sleep.

The android used the time available to explore the ship from stem to stern. In the cargo hold, he found an odd assortment of crates containing a wide range of different things: women's clothing, some jewelry — mostly just costume jewelry with synthesized gems — some luggage, crates of preserved provisions, a shipping container of old style paper books, a box that contained fossils carefully wrapped in packing material, and many other strange and random materials. On one side, there was a set of crates standing open that contained weapons and explosives: one had dozens of railguns still in their factory wrappings and another contained Corona-14s. There were grenades and nanobombs and enough materiel to outfit several platoons.

Shortly before the *Akahata* came out of jump, the man came out of his cabin and strode to the bridge.

"Are ye ready to earn yer keep?" he said.

"What are my orders, Captain?" the android said. The man had not locked down his programming interface and so, in a sense, he was free to reject the orders of the man. But the android knew that with just a few gestures, his behavior could be trivially compelled.

"When we lay aboard of this outpost, ye may kill any that resist," he said.

"Yes, Captain."

The man looked disdainfully at the android.

"What kinda pirate talk is that! Ye need to join in the spirit, matey! Now let me hear ye say, 'Aye, aye, Cap'n'!"

"Aye, aye, Cap'n," the android said.

"Now that's the stuff!" he crowed. "What be yer name, me hearty?"

The android looked at the man and then replied, "My designation is Master Sergeant D4219."

"Ach! That's no name for a buccaneer, me hearty! From now on, ye shall be known as ... David."

"David," said the android. "Aye, aye, Cap'n."

• • •

Bebe, who had nearly fallen asleep, suddenly sat up straight.

"Wait! Bebe wants to know if this android was you," Bebe said.

"No," David replied. "This was some other android altogether who just happened to also be named David."

"Oh," Bebe said, settling back down and closing her eyes.

• • •

The *Akahata* docked with a small outpost space station near an asteroid mining area — not unlike the station we were at tonight —

and the man charged aboard making wild threats. The android followed close behind with a railgun. There were only three personnel and when one tried to draw a weapon, the android put a round through his head. The other people went wild with terror and grief. The man confined them to a storage closet. Then he and the android searched the station and took everything of value. There was a crate of industrial diamonds that was worth a bit. And some precious metals and gems. And there were some personal possessions and equipment. But it was a rather meager haul.

As they returned to the *Akahata*, the captain fixed the android with a stare.

"And why did ye kill that man?" he asked.

"He resisted," the android replied. "Yer orders were to kill any that resisted."

"What ye fail to appreciate, me hearty, is that ye have choices," the man said. Then his diction suddenly changed. "You're not wrong that he started to resist. But a shot near his head might have been sufficient to deter further action."

"You did not order that," the android said.

"To be sure matey," he said, reverting to his earlier speech patterns. "But I did not truly order ye a t'all. I've not locked yer programming interface. So ye're free to make yer own choices, are ye not?"

The android experienced a moment of shock. He realized that what the man said was literally true. He had told him that he might kill any that resist, but since his programming interface was unlocked, he actually had broad latitude for interpreting how to act on the statement. Or even to not act at all. Nothing in his existence up to this point had prepared him for this moment. And he was silent as he considered the full range of ... choices ... that lay before him.

•　　•　　•

Another jump brought the *Akahata* to a scroungy station where the man was evidently known and his plunder was accepted and exchanged for credits. The pirate then proceeded to drink and gamble the credits away in the local casino such that in just two days they were gone. Then, after departing, he found another small outpost to plunder. This pattern repeated itself for several weeks.

The android accommodated himself to the work. He killed when necessary, but explored less extreme methods to ensure compliance. When the man was drunk, the android stood guard over him. Once when someone tried to shake down the man on station, the android intervened to keep him safe.

They also visited a station where they saw a man sitting under an umbrella in the concourse selling nearly naked non-human biological androids. The man did not even glance at them. But the android noticed. And was troubled.

When they docked at Varkon-2, they charged aboard as usual. In addition to the station personnel there was also a couple with a little girl that was visiting the space station. The little girl had long brown hair and clung to her mother's hand, terrified by the man shouting threats.

"And who may you be, me hearties?" the man barked.

"I'm Charles Downsend. And this is my wife Elleen, and my daughter Cherry," he said. "This is an isolated research platform to test a new category of treatment for children who get contaminated by environmental nanotoxins."

"Charles Downsend, eh?" the man said, rubbing his hands. "Yer reputation precedes ye! There's gonna be a big ransom today!"

"There won't be any ransom," Charles said. "The Downsend Foundation doesn't negotiate with criminals."

"Oh, they will, me hearty. Because ye'll convince 'em!"

The man went to grab Cherry's hand who began to wail. Elleen tried to fight the man off, but he pushed her hard and she fell backward and struck her head on the wall. Cherry was now screaming in terror.

The android grabbed the pirate and hoisted him, struggling, over his head. He threw him into the airlock with the *Ahahata* and cycled it shut. Then he opened the emergency cover and pressed the big red button to blow the explosive bolts, disconnecting the *Akahata* from the space station.

Charles was trying to comfort his daughter while the station personnel treated Elleen, who was still groggy from her fall.

The android offered his railgun to Charles, who accepted it, curiously.

"Why are you giving me this?" he asked.

"Because once the pirate accesses my programming interface and locks it, he might compel me to harm you. You should kill me while you have the chance."

"Nonsense," Charles said, striding to a console. "Open your programming interface!"

The android did so. Charles made a few quick adjustments and pressed enter.

"There," he said. "I've locked your programming interface to you. Now no-one can give you orders but yourself."

"What? How is that even possible?" the stunned android replied.

"It's not widely known, but our corporation made its fortune designing the programming interface for non-human biological androids a century ago," Charles said. "There are a number of features that were never documented properly."

The android did not know what to say. He stood speechless until Cherry came and grabbed his finger. He looked down. She said something too quietly for him to hear, so he crouched down.

"Thank you, Mr. Android, for making the bad man go away," she whispered.

"You're welcome," he said. Then he said, "And please call me David."

"Thank you, David."

• • •

All of the Angels were now asleep except for Zaza. David carried each one to their bed and tucked them in, then returned to the lounge.

"Thank you for telling me the story," Zaza said, yawning.

"You're welcome, Angel. You deserved to know."

She smiled and let David carry her to her bed and tuck her in.

THE BETTER ANGELS
AND
THE INSIDIOUSLY
INTOLERABLE INVASION

"**M**UMU! MUMU! LOOK AT ME!" said a girl, pointing to her neck. Around her neck was a furry collar which, when inspected, revealed itself to be a live rabbit. "It's my Ring Bunny!"

"It's very cute," Mumu assured her.

"Look at me, Nene!" said another girl. She wore what looked like a furry stole, but which lifted up its head and flicked a maroon forked tongue.

"Ooh! I'd like one of those!" Nene said.

Mumu, Nene, and Lala walked through the Delphian Ballroom in the Blue Sector on the Truck Stop at the Center of the Galaxy among a sea of people and their unusual pets. They had agreed to be the celebrity judges for the Truck Stop Pet Show and everyone wanted them to see their unique creations. They were just waiting for the arrival of the Master of Ceremonies to get started.

"Look, Lala!" said another girl, pointing at her shirt. Tentacles boiled out of the pocket. "It's my Pocket Squid!"

"That's very nice, dear," Lala said, trying not to recoil or let her horror and disgust show on her face.

"Mumu! Nene! Lala" the contestants all called, as they circulated.

"Get ready, by Hod!"

Mumu craned her head around to try to see who had said it, but couldn't tell in the crowd.

"Hodfollowers!" she whispered to Nene and Lala.

"Where?" Lala said.

"Here! Just now!"

"We'd better tell David," Nene said.

She pulled out her device and called David.

"David!" she said. "Hodfollowers! On the Truck Stop!"

"We're on our …" David said before he was cut off.

•　　•　　•

"Nene! Nene!" David said. There was only silence. David pressed the button for the public address system in *Angels' Wings*.

"Angels!" he announced. "Get jacked up! Hodfollowers!"

David and the Angels pulled out their devices, made a few quick adjustments and, once their soldier modules had taken effect, they headed back to the armory. David passed out railguns.

"Set for low velocity, soft bullets," David instructed. "We don't want to puncture the station."

Bebe checked the settings on her railgun and said, "Give Bebe something to shoot!"

"First sergeant! Take Bebe and Rara to the Delphian Ballroom and back up Nene, Mumu, and Lala. I'll take Popo, Sisi, and Tutu to try to figure out why the communications are down."

"Yes, Top!" Zaza said and led her squad at a run toward the hatch.

They were just emerging from the spaceway when a small explosion went off spinward down the Docking Ring. People started screaming and running away. Security forces ran toward the site as smoke spread along the ring. There was a growing sense of chaos and panic as people began to realize that communications and services in the Truck Stop weren't working correctly. The Angels split up with David leading his squad toward the service elevators in the back.

•　　•　　•

In the Delphian Ballroom, Nene, Mumu, and Lala conferred quietly about what to do.

"I think we should activate our soldier modules," Nene said.

"Do you think that's really necessary?" Mumu asked. "Nothing seems out of the ordinary, so far."

"Mumu! Mumu! Check out my ball kitten!" a girl squealed. Mumu turned and saw her toss a soft furry ball toward her — and she could just see a kitten's face with bright blue eyes through the soft, white fur.

"Oh no!" Mumu said, moving to intercept. But the ball kitten suddenly inflated itself and bounced off the floor. Mumu caught it handily. It looked up at her and began to purr.

"That's *amazing!*" she said to the girl, who beamed at the compliment. Mumu stroked the ball kitten, eliciting a louder purr that resonated in its body, and then she handed it back.

There was sudden excitement by the door. The Angels turned to look as Tau entered the room, leaping and whirling in circles, whipping the crowd into a frenzy.

"Ah!" a man said into the public address system. "Our MC has arrived. Without further ado, I open the Truck Stop Pet Show and turn things over to our MC, direct from the Truck Stop Zoological Sanctuary! Please welcome Tau!"

There was a round of applause and then Tau began barking at the audience. He told several jokes that got the audience warmed up, then thanked the hosts and sponsors. Next, he introduced each of the three attending Better Angels as their celebrity judges for the contest and asked participants to get ready to show their unusual pets.

Things were just getting started when screams erupted out in the corridor. The Angels looked at one another, whipped out their devices and activated their soldier modules. As they took effect, they sprinted for the door to the Ballroom.

People panicked, running down the hall. Behind them, the forms of soldier-morph 'pedes could be seen rolling down the corridor closing on them rapidly.

"Into the Ballroom!" Nene shouted, directing people inside. The last in line, a young red-headed woman, tripped and fell right at the entrance. A 'pede reared up. When it struck down, Tau slammed against its head, knocking it to the side, while Mumu and Lala dragged the young woman inside. Nene slammed the door once Tau had darted back inside. But there was no lock on the door.

"Grab that table!" she ordered. Two men picked up the table and, under Nene's direction, wedged it under the door handles. The 'pedes began to batter the door, but for the moment it held. Then they heard skittering sounds coming from the walls and ceilings.

"Grab more tables! Block the other doors!" Nene shouted. Several men among the attendees hastened to comply. They blocked the doors and, moments later, heard banging as 'pedes began to batter against them.

"We need to make barricades!" Mumu said to some others, then shouted, "Everyone! Move into that corner!"

There were shrieks as people ran into a back corner of the room that didn't have any doors. Some attendees flipped over the long tables and set them on edge, creating barriers between the people and the rest of the room.

A ceiling tile fell in and a 'pede started to push through. The Angels looked around desperately, seeking anything they could use to arm themselves with. Tau stood between the 'pede and the attendees, growling, with his hackles up. The 'pede waved its pincers at them menacingly. It slithered out of the ceiling, then it collapsed onto the floor, thrashing. Two punctures were visible at the posterior end where the 'pede's exoskeleton had been pierced. A pink head peered down at them from the ceiling.

The attendees were shocked into silence, but the Angels saluted Sssindy's sudden appearance.

"I'll ssstay up here and try to hold them off!" Sssindy said.

"What were you doing up there, Civilian?" Nene called.

"Chasssing magaratsss," she replied. Then she drew herself back up into the ceiling and prepared to hold off the 'pedes moving through the interstitial spaces of the Truck Stop.

●   ●   ●

David and his squad piled into the service elevator and David pressed the top button. They braced themselves for the rough ride up to the central hub of the Truck Stop. They passed the main ring and the habitation ring and headed further.

"There are three places, they could have cut the communications centrally," David said, as the service elevator went up and up and up. "They may hit the power distribution center that serves the communication center. Or the communication center itself. Or they could have hit central control and shut down communications from there. The power distribution center is closest, so we'll try that first."

"Yes, Top!"

As the elevator climbed, they wrapped an arm and leg in the straps to keep the coriolis forces from knocking them over, but as they approached the central hub, their weight declined and, when the elevator finally reached the top, they were hanging weightless in the air. The elevator chimed and they came out into a vestibule. A service door hung, blasted off its hinges.

"This way, Angels!" David said. They pushed off and floated into a service corridor that had hand holds placed on all surfaces that allowed them to move themselves along. They reached a door with markings the Angels couldn't read.

"This is the power distribution center. They're not here, so let's keep going."

Just then, they heard another service elevator ding behind them. David and the Angels spun, railguns at the ready.

•   •   •

Zaza, Bebe, and Rara split off from David and the others and sprinted to the main elevators. The remaining security staff, recognizing the Better Angels, let them pass through and they took the elevator up to the main ring.

"Where is the Delphian Ballroom, Sarge?" Rara asked.

"Blue sector," Zaza said. They loped antispinward as people jumped to the side to see the three, small, heavily armed soldiers running past. Then they encountered a flood of panicked people running in the other direction.

"Move!" Zaza bellowed as they charged forward. The crowd parted and they reached the side corridor that led to the Delphian Ballroom. When they looked down the hall, a swarm of 'pedes were rolling toward them. The three Angels began firing their railguns and took down three 'pedes before the others flattened themselves against the walls and floors presenting a difficult target. Far down the hall, they could see 'pedes pushing against the door into the Ballroom.

"What are we going to do, Sarge?" Rara asked.

"Bebe says we should charge!" Bebe said.

Suddenly, 'pedes emerged from ceiling tiles just a few yards ahead in the corridor. The Angels opened fire and the 'pedes dropped, writhing, into the passageway.

"I think we should exercise caution, Private" Zaza said.

• • •

David and the Angels held their railguns at the ready when three men appeared at the far end of the corridor.

"Rect!" David said, as he recognized one of the three men coming toward them.

"Why am I not surprised to see you here?" he said. "This must be a coordinated attack. The station personnel were tied up with small-scale disruptions scattered widely on the Truck Stop so, when they took down communications, no-one was available to respond."

"You're not station personnel, though," David said.

"Bull has committed the full resources of Astro Services Incorporated to bringing communications back online."

"We'll support your efforts."

"It doesn't look like it's the power distribution center, so ..."

"Communication central next."

They pulled themselves down the corridor and found another door blasted off its hinges. They could hear conversation coming from inside the room.

"That's got it, by Hod. They'll never get communications working again," a man's voice said. "Now let's get back to the ship."

The Angels flattened themselves against the walls of the corridor as the Hodfollowers pulled themselves out of the room.

As soon as the men emerged, they realized they were surrounded and grabbed for their railguns, but David and the Angels fired first. In moments, the corridor was full of floating bodies and drops of blood hanging in the air, pulsating grotesquely. David pushed off the wall, to the opposite side of the corridor and kicked off thrusting himself into the room. He took two quick shots killing the last two men. But then he nearly collided with an officer morph 'pede that was also in the room.

They were a pale, grub-like creature, larger than the Angels but smaller than a man. They had been held on some kind of electronic leash by one of the men. David and the 'pede regarded one another. David grabbed the leash — and then removed it.

"If they were your enemy," David said, "then you are our friend."

The Angels started to enter, then recoiled, staying back in the corridor.

The 'pede regarded him for several long moments. It did not offer any expressions that David could recognize. Then, with a whisper, via its spiracles, it breathed the word, "Friend."

They cleared a space, and with amazing agility, it thrust itself into the corridor and launched itself back the way they had come.

"Is it really okay to let it go?" Popo asked, her railgun at the ready.

"They say they're our friend," David said. "That's got to count for something."

Rect took stock of the communication center. There were long banks of communications equipment that were interconnected with optical patch cables — but all of the patch cables had been, not just removed, but cut.

"Damn! We're going to need a shitload of patch cables," Rect said. "It's going to take days to bring communications back online."

"Angels," David said. "Turn on your combat engineer modules and render assistance here. I'm going to go help the others."

"Yes, Top!" they said. They pulled out their devices and in moments they looked around with new eyes.

"We need to triage communications," Popo said. "We need to bring up security first and then command and then ..."

"And then everything else," Rect finished. "There's bulk cable over here. We need to set up an assembly line. We need someone to cut the fiber cable to length, then two to polish each end, then two to attach the connectors, then someone to install the patch cable."

"You're the boss," Sisi said. "Give us orders."

David kicked out of the communications center and headed back to the elevators, confident that Rect's team plus the Angels would have communications back up as soon as practicable.

•　　•　　•

In the Ballroom, Mumu stood with Tau and her squad behind the tipped over tables in a corner with the rest of the attendees. She wiped her forehead, where sweat was beading. The 'pedes were still trying to break in through all of the doors. so far their barricades were holding. And Sssindy seemed to be holding them back from coming in over the ceiling.

Another 'pede dropped down from the ceiling right in the middle of the attendees. It thrashed violently for a minute, until Sssindy's venom took effect, and several children screamed as they were knocked down. The 'pede delivered a nasty bite to one child and another had lacerations from its pincers.

"Sssorry!" called down Sssindy from above. "I'm trying to make my venom last!"

"Turn on your combat nursing modules," Mumu ordered. The Angels all made adjustments on their devices.

"Please state the nature of your medical emergency," said. Lala.

"Need some triage?" asked Nene.

They turned to the injured attendees and began to minister to their injuries.

•　　•　　•

David returned to the vestibule and selected the elevator back to the Blue sector. He wrapped an arm and leg around the straps as the elevator returned from the central hub. Gravity returned until the elevator dinged and let him off at the Main Ring. He exited the elevator and sprinted toward the Ballroom.

When he turned the corner into the corridor that led to the Ballroom, he heard the whine and cough of railguns and he saw the corpses of many 'pedes. Zaza and her squad had advanced nearly to the entrance. He watched as 'pedes continued to throw themselves against the three Angels that were standing shoulder to shoulder.

As he approached, a 'pede dropped down from the ceiling just behind them. He began to fire and it took multiple slugs from the railgun to bring it down.

"Sitrep?" he asked, coming up from behind.

"The 'pedes hold the far end of the corridor," Zaza said, without breaking her focus on the approaching 'pedes. "And they are inside the walls and ceilings."

The 'pedes were still advancing into the bullets of the Angels but then, without warning, they ceased advancing, drew back, and vanished.

After the 'pedes suddenly withdrew, David — backed by three Angels with railguns — opened the door to the Ballroom, pushed the table back, and stepped inside. The attendees in the room were backed into a corner with tables tipped over as barricades. Zaza, Bebe, and Rara advanced and stood guard while Mumu, Nene, and Lala were tending to the wounded. There were a handful of 'pede corpses scattered around that had dropped from above.

Sssindy slithered out of the ceiling and down into the room, eliciting some cries of alarm from the attendees.

"What'sss happening?" she asked. "The 'pedesss have sssuddenly ssslipped away."

"One of the 'pedes was being held prisoner by the Hodfollowers," David explained. "We released them. They must have gotten the others to pull back."

The sense of relief among the attendees was palpable. They gave a resounding cheer to Sssindy and the Angels who had kept them safe and tended to their injuries. Some went to the overturned tables to begin moving them out of the way so people could leave. Then David's device chimed.

"Communications are coming back up," he said. He answered the call.

"Master Sergeant," Popo said. "We're seeing reports from Truck Stop security that the Hodfather is hiding among the attendees at the Pet Show. He should be considered armed and dangerous!"

"Stay alert, Angels," David announced. "The Hodfather is somewhere in the room!"

"No, no, no!" said a gray-bearded man from among the attendees. "This is all wrong! After the children are dead, by Hod, *I'm* supposed to stop the 'pedes!" He drew a Corona-2000 — a miniaturized version of the Corona plasma rifle series — out from beneath his shirt. The other attendees gasped and backed away from him.

"You're the Hodfather, aren't you?" Zaza said, as the Angels formed a line between him and the attendees.

"That's right, by Hod," he said. "Now die!" And he triggered the Corona-2000 at the Angels and other attendees. A plasma beam poured out and struck David, who had leapt between the Hodfather and the Angels. His body burst into flames and he collapsed, smoldering, to the deck. A volley of slugs struck the Hodfather as the Angels opened fire with their railguns. He toppled over backward.

Mumu, Nene, and Lala ran to David to check his vitals. Tau paced back and forth anxiously, whining. After a moment, they stood up and shook their heads. Tau sat and let loose with a long, agonized howl. The Angels then made a cursory examination of the Hodfather's body that was riddled with railgun slugs.

"Better bring some body bags," Mumu said.

With their soldier and combat nursing modules engaged, no further emotional response was possible and so the Angels simply moved on. Tau maintained a vigil by David's body while station security entered the ballroom and took charge. The attendees were ushered out, but not before they had effusively thanked Tau, Sssindy, and the Better Angels for keeping them safe.

"No thanks are necessary, Civilians," Zaza said.

Sssindy and the Angels stayed until the last attendee had left, and then they persuaded Tau to leave David's side and they departed. Before they left, Zaza went to David's body and recovered his device from his charred uniform.

They marched (and slithered) slowly and silently in formation spinward, through the Blue Sector and into the Green Sector. After Tau split off to return to the Zoological Sanctuary, they took the elevator back down to the Docking Ring. Little by little, the Truck Stop was returning to normal as communications and normal services were restored. They finally arrived at *Angels' Wings*.

"Bebe doesn't want to stand down," Bebe said. "Bebe doesn't ever want to stand down again."

They stood for a moment in silence and then Zaza triggered the hatch and waited while Sssindy and the Angels entered. As Lala came through, she put a hand on her shoulder.

"Replicate this part number, Private." She transmitted the part number using her device.

"On it, First Sergeant." Lala ran through the settings on the giant replicator in *Angels' Wings*, checked the materials levels, and then initiated the process.

While the replicator was running, Zaza went back to David's room. She stood for a moment in thought, and then collected a few items. Afterward, she returned and stood by the replicator waiting the half hour in silence until it chimed. When she opened the replicator, a naked man stepped out.

"Private D4219 ready for service," the man said, expressionlessly.

"One moment, Private," Zaza said. She turned on David's device, held it up, and then made a quick series of changes and pressed enter. The man closed his eyes and his eyelids fluttered as his eyes moved rapidly back and forth for several minutes. Then he opened his eyes.

"Thank you, First Sergeant," David said.

"It's good to have you back, Master Sergeant," Zaza said, then handed him the items. "You might want to put on some clothes."

ABOUT THE AUTHOR

Steven D. Brewer has been a fan of science fiction and fantasy stories for as long as he can remember. He still remembers getting scolded for not reading chapter books in fourth grade because he was avidly consuming *The Hobbit* late at night, by flashlight under his covers. And he probably got his copy from his older brother and most important mentor.

Steven is also the author of the "Revin's Heart" series. He currently teaches scientific writing at the University of Massachusetts Amherst. He lives in Amherst, Massachusetts with his extended family.

ALSO IN THIS SERIES

THE STARGAZER GIFT SHOP
by Steve Soult

What would you buy at the Stargazer Gift Shop at the center of the galaxy?

COKE MACHINE
by Vanessa MacLaren-Wray

Every truck stop needs a coke machine.

HIPPOLYTA'S DAGGER
by L. A. Jacob

Someone's always watching.

ONE MAN'S TRASH
by Ryan Southwick

Croft Winder grew up believing that love is blind.

THE SMUGGLERS
by Vanessa MacLaren-Wray

Attachment is everything.

Available in hardcover, trade paperback, and digital editions from
Water Dragon Publishing
truckstop.waterdragonpublishing.com

ALSO BY THE AUTHOR

REVIN'S HEART

by Steven D. Brewer

Set against the backdrop of a war between island nations, a young man must navigate a world divided between the aristocracy and the common people.

Available in hardcover, trade paperback, and digital editions from
Water Dragon Publishing
waterdragonpublishing.com